CW01390754

OUR LADY OF THE SNOWS

ALSO BY JAMES BUCHAN

FICTION

A Parish of Rich Women

Davy Chadwick

Slide

Heart's Journey in Winter

High Latitudes: A Romance

A Good Place to Die

The Gate of Air

The Family of William Neilson

Book I, A Street Shaken by Light

Book II, A Chalice Argent

NON-FICTION

Jeddah: Old and New

Frozen Desire: An Enquiry into the Meaning of Money

Capital of the Mind: How Edinburgh Changed the World

Adam Smith and the Pursuit of Perfect Liberty

Days of God: The Revolution in Iran and Its Consequences

John Law: A Scottish Adventurer of the Eighteenth Century

THE FAMILY OF WILLIAM NEILSON BOOK III

OUR LADY OF THE SNOWS

James Buchan

First published in Great Britain in 2025 by
Mountain Leopard Press
An imprint of HEADLINE PUBLISHING GROUP LIMITED

1

Cataloguing in Publication Data is available from the British Library

Hardback ISBN 978 1 8006 9916 8

Typeset in Adobe Caslon Pro 11.5pt/16.4pt by Jouve (UK), Milton Keynes

Printed and bound in Great Britain by Clays Ltd, Elcograf S.p.A.

Headline's policy is to use papers that are natural, renewable and recyclable products and made from wood grown in well-managed forests and other controlled sources. The logging and manufacturing processes are expected to conform to the environmental regulations of the country of origin.

HEADLINE PUBLISHING GROUP LIMITED
An Hachette UK Company
Carmelite House
50 Victoria Embankment
London EC4Y 0DZ

The authorised representative in the EEA is Hachette Ireland, 8 Castlecourt Centre, Dublin 15, D15 XTP3, Ireland (email: info@hbgi.ie)

www.headline.co.uk
www.hachette.co.uk

CONTENTS

Peu de gens savent être vieux
Few people know how to be old

Duc de La Rochefoucauld

Author's Note: *Powattamie's speech on pages 111–113 is taken, all but word for word, from that of Le Serpent Piqué (Tattooed Snake) at Natchez in 1723 or 1724, as recorded by his friend A.-S. Le Page du Pratz.*

PART I

La Ferté-Joyeuse, 1754

I

There is, I believe, no enterprise of man and woman so fatal to the harmony of the married condition as a scheme of hydraulic engineering gone awry; and the more so when it is the lady who pays for the works.

"You are absent this night, husband," Mme Neilson said on an evening of the spring of 1754, after our children had risen from table. "I have lost the Scottish chatter-box that revived an icy French heart."

"Forgive me, madame," I said. "I am much engaged. There is some difficulty with Lock No. 7."

"Is that the work at La Berthinerie? I cannot keep pace with your excavations."

"Yes, madame. I am at a stand with the entire reach from the Ferme de La Berthinerie to that of Les Roseaux."

I waited, so as to permit Mme Neilson the maximum of pleasure in my failure.

She said: "In truth, dear friend, I am not as surprised as I should be. When you first brought me the canal project, I had the most lively doubts, but, in a flush of feminine passion, where I wished only to please you, I submitted to your judgment. Now that that passion is consolidated into esteem, I find my former conduct inexplicable. Not for a moment, sir, do I blame you."

"Madame, your passion may have abated. Mine has not and never shall. It is simply that the *strata* are much harder to work than I had reckoned. The gravels will not hold the water."

"I am sure you have applied mortar to the base of the channel, embedded oak sleepers into the cement and lined the elevations with brick."

"Yes, madame."

"Would it help you, dear friend, if I made a visit of inspection to your works?"

"I believe it would help me exceedingly."

II

Of all my bad ideas, the Canal de Madame was the worst.

On the top of my fiftieth year, I had lived a daft,

vagabonding sort of life. Bred up in Edinburgh, I had come into France in 1720 at the age of sixteen to serve as commis or clerk at the bank established at Paris by my countryman, Mr John Law of Lauriston. I brought that gentleman no good fortune, for the bank stopped payment on the day of my appearance, but not before I had seen, in the shareholders' gallery, a young girl in Court dress who treated me with kindness. Though quite the least of Mr Law's servants, I was held liable for a portion of the bank's debts and lodged, at His Christian Majesty's pleasure, for six years in the castle of the Bastille. My world shrank to four icy walls. The only memento of my life as a free man was a handkerchief the young lady had given me at the Bank.

Freed for no wiser reason than that for which I had been imprisoned, I was indentured to the French India Company to go as a writer to its factory in Chandernagore in Bengale. I never saw that place. The vessel transporting me, the *Prince-de-Conty*, wrecked on the coast of the île de France or Mauritius. I alone survived. At Port-Louis, the chief settlement of that forlorn island, I found my friend married to the Governor of the island, M. le marquis de Maurepas, and not especially glad to see me. Desirous to be quit of me (or so I thought), Mme de Maurepas shipped me in irons to Pondicherry.

I passed eighteen years in India and Persia, sometimes in mercenary soldiering, sometimes in native diplomacy. My singular good fortune was to be held captive for a season in the late war by a young English officer, Captain Edmund Harris. Although we served different masters, we became loving friends.

In the year 1745, I was ordered to return to the metropolis for the particular service of His Christian Majesty. Stopping at Port-Louis for our captain to take on vittal and water, I learned that M. Maurepas had died and his widow returned to her lands in Mother France. Debarking at Lorient in Brittany, I was directed to attend Charles Stuart, exiled Prince of Wales, who had carried an army into Scotland and was then at Inverness.

I was present, on April 16th, 1746, at the fight on Culloden Moor, where, by an incompetent manoeuvre, I destroyed my entire command. I might have remained on that bloody moor, my gallant Irish soldiers blown to pieces and my ankles broken by round shot, had not Providence, in the shape of Mr Harris, wisked me away into safety. Conscious as granite, I was carried to the Western Isles. A privateer from Dunkerque, M. Douvry, swept me up off a beach on the isle of Barray, carried the pieces to his home port, stacked them on a good horse and pointed the beast at the desert district of France called La Sologne. Always attentive to affairs, M. Douvry must have judged that his best prospect of recovering his costs and a reasonable profit was by application to the open-handed Mme de Maurepas.

When I came to my senses, I found myself in the castle of La Ferté-Joyeuse and the place in uproar: my lady dying of the small-pox and her neighbours debauching her servants and cutting at her lands.

With the help of God and a system of surgery I had learned in Persia, I cured Mme de Maurepas of her evil distemper.

During my convalessing, I was attended by a young kitchen servant, a foundling from the hospital in Orléans named by the good sisters Marie-Ange de la Contrition. We became friends. Mme de Maurepas was expert in all fields of scientific and philosophical enquiry. When I proposed a general inoculation against the small-pox, such as I had witnessed in my travels in Persia, that lady consented. Her servants and tenants distrusted the treatment, which was not then widespread in France, but the little servant-girl stepped forward and her bravery shamed her elders into compliance.

My presence in the house was disagreeable not only to my lady's Intendant, M. Ballin, who was robbing his mistress, but also to the lady's nephew, M. le comte de Luynes, who believed he had holy right to her succession: *viz.* the castle and its policies; a hôtel particulier in Paris, rue Varenne; fifty-eight farms; a gallery of Venetian pictures in the very best taste; a library of eighty thousand volumes; and several millions in the French and English stocks. M. Luynes was determined that his aunt should die a widow.

Rather than challenge me, M. Luynes hired ruffians to murder my orphan-friend in the hope of giving me the scares. The diligence of my lady's huntsman, M. Duclos, foiled the scheme. The hunt servants without and I within chased the Frondeurs and put the fear of God into my lady's neighbours. M. Luynes I had intended to fight, but Mme de Maurepas over-rode me, and exiled the fop to Louisiana. Since then, we had had no report of him and it was my holy wish that he had fallen foul of the Chickasas or Cheroquie and given his body to the swamps and his soul up to its Maker as ineligible for commerce.

For my assistance in this bustle, I received in reward my lady's hand in marriage and, about the same time, or a little before, a son whom she named in my honour William. Mlle Marie-Ange de la Contrition my lady adopted as her god-daughter and heiress. The child was addressed as Mlle de Joyeuse.

I was not especially eager to return to the active service of His Very Christian Majesty. I had become one of his military officers not out of devotion to the kingdom of France, the Roman Catholic cult or the cause of the Jacobites in England and Scotland (which last I detested), but for the love of the lady who had become my wife.

Being of an active disposition, I proposed to Mme Neilson the digging of a canal to drain the bottom lands of her property, to convey marl from pits in the Pays Fort to the east with which to cure the sour soil, and to open a communication to the more distant farms. In place of their meagre harvests of rye, her tenants might sow wheat and turn out their beasts into clover. With a single scheme, so I believed, Mme Neilson would remedy both the sterility of Solognot earth and the insalubrity of Solognot air. Should the King ever see fit to unite the Loire and the Cher across the width of the Sologne, from Combleux to Selles or Sully to Vierzon, a laborious up-and-down traverse I deemed beyond my capacities and my lady's purse, a junction canal would open to her farmers extended markets at Tours, Nantes and the Atlantic ports.

The project presented to first sight no great difficulty. Unlike the famous Canal du Midi, cut in the great King's reign to unite the rivers Garonne and Aude at a junction to the south of Toulouse, the canal would pass down just a single river basin, that of the Sauldre. There would be no requirement for a reservoir at the watershed between two drainages, or what we call a *bief de partage*. The declination was slight, a matter of but two hundred feet over fifteen leagues, and would require at most twenty-three locks and weirs to hold back the water.

I had found in my lady's library a manuscript project of Leonardo of Vinci, from that great savant's residence at Fontainebleau, that I adapted but did not improve. The head of the canal I fixed at Blancafort. Two burns, the Oizenette at Argent, and the Nère at Clémont, would supply tributary water to the upper reaches. It being peace-time, the King of France graciously put at Mme Neilson's disposition the Champagne regiment, then doing very little at all at Orléans. There followed two years of labour, frustration, bickers with neighbours and mill-owners, smashed limbs, pillage, desertion, palustrine fevers, dis-senterie and expense without limit.

I rode myself saddle-sore with young William in croupe the whole trace of the canal, many times. The miller at Blancafort, M. Opine, did all he could, this side assassination, to frustrate me. Though I would be taking the waters of the river downstream of his mill, he refused to allow me to measure the flow of water, and begrutched even a wine-bottle of the nectar for Mme Neilson to make analysis of its *limonage* or calcareous element. The bonnet lairds and other small gentlemen said I would raise winter wages in the district, and the people might – God forbid! – have bread to eat. The arrival of the advance party of the King's soldiers caused them to sulk.

Beneath the bad sands of the Sologne is an impermeable *stratum* or pann of slate. One has but to excavate a ditch for it to fill with water. A boot-print may still be traced a year later. I believed that the canal would lose water from the passage of boats through the locks, and from evaporation off the surface, but not from infiltration or leakage. Alas! Downstream of the town of Argent, we came on a gravelly and permeable matrice that would not hold water. The depth of the canal in the dry months would here come down just one foot or none at all. The mills on the Sauldre upstream of the head held back, and released, their water without regularity but always with malice. Who would have known that a lock, just fifteen toises in length and one in depth, every time it was filled and opened to let a loaded barge bump through, could be so reckless with God's water!

Back in 'Forty-seven, I had thrown into one of the million ponds of the country a diamond so precious it might dig a dozen of canals. The property of King James Stuart of England, Scotland and Ireland, it was given by that unhappy prince, after our defeat on Culloden Moor, to Mme Neilson. She ordered me to be put the diamond beyond all human reach lest it be sold and the proceeds used to embody a new Jacobite army and send it to ruin in Scotland. The jewel glittered at me from its watery bed. The curse of my youth, the evil object leered over my middling years.

III

The inspection of the works was to be without notice or, rather, as I improved Mme Neilson's order, with warning of just five days. Our head camp was erected some five or six miles upstream from the castle. My lady, who did not care to ride horses, took coach while I trotted along with my children. Mlle de Joyeuse was in excellent mood.

"The brigadier is in disgrace."

"No! Not you, too, my darling."

"Why is Papa in disgrace?" My son disliked family discord.

"He has thrown Maman's fortune into a hole in the ground."

Mlle de Joyeuse pricked her horse, and cantered to the carriage, where she appeared to be talking to Mme Neilson through the glasses.

Young William touched my bridle hand. "Do not fear, Father. My sister will find my mother's money."

Which she did.

IV

For all the short advertisement, the men had erected a tent for Mme Neilson's reception. Wisps of steam from above the roof-pins and the scent of roasted mutton hinted that the officers did not expect feminine questions long to postpone a military feast. They were deceived. Mme Neilson descended in boots, put up her veil, declined refreshment. I presented the gentlemen. An adjutant was detached to accompany our children on a pleasure-party, while Mme Neilson and I set off, on foot, with the regimental commander, Colonel de Morne. His officers, uncertain whether to follow riches or beauty, divided into two. The fires beneath the kettles were damped down.

As we proceeded, at snail's pace, we were buffetted, every now and then, by the shock of detonation which caused Mme Neilson's veil to flutter. Thunder rolled and scuttled about us.

Mme Neilson halted. She said: "Colonel Morne, the purpose of this project of canalisation is to furnish an inheritance for the Chevalier Neilson and Mlle de Joyeuse. It shall defeat itself if the legatees will have been strewn in pieces over the Generality."

M. Morne turned to his officers but they were giving spur to their mounts, every one of them. It seems they had come to regret their election and wished, under the pretext of halting the pyrotechnica, to share in Mlle de Joyeuse's company. M. Morne was purple with rage and mortification.

Mme Neilson touched that officer's sleeve. "Colonel Morne, there is no greater reward for a lady than to be outshone by her daughter . . ."

". . . or for a father by his son."

These words wrought a revolution in the colonel. He peeped at Mme Neilson and saw she was a human being: a human being of property but a human being withal. With but two auditors, his manner changed. Where he had been short in his answers, even impatient, he became full and frank. He made no attempt to simplify the obstacles thrown up by the engineering, for he saw that there was no need. There followed a festival of trigonometry, always to Mme Neilson's taste. M. Morne spoke, for the first time, of his fear of failure. By the time we returned to camp, the fires had been lit again. I was hungry fit to eat grass.

The tables were set in a rectangular, with at the top a

transverse board to accommodate the proprietors. As we took station, there was a tumulte at the further end. My children came in, amid officers talking all over one another. Mlle de Joyeuse thanked her escorts in general, passed her whip to her brother, walked to the head and took up position behind her god-mother's right shoulder. Mme Neilson did not turn to her but stood, if that might be possible, a little more the upright. A ghost of fatigue or weariness that I had not marked in my wife became evident only in its disappearance. I had not known till then what fortification Mme Neilson received from her goddaughter. The Chevalier stood behind my left shoulder, stinking of gunpowder. Had he brushed a candle, he would have exploded.

A glass of Champagne was placed at Mme Neilson's elbow, but she did not touch it, or the two others that succeeded it at intervals during her discourse.

"Gentlemen," she said, "I have this morning, by tiresome feminine questions, and their patient answers, acquired a more precise notion of the scale of this project of canalisation and of the obstacles placed by Nature and our own frailty in its path. Mr Neilson and M. Morne have led me to understand that there are two principal difficulties: the reach between the locks designed "7" and "8" and the flow of water in the dry season in the upper stages.

Further, I understand that those elements are like links in a chain. Should one or t'other fail, then fails the whole.

"The matter of the reach at La Berthinerie is quickly disposed. Nothing outside heaven will bring back your labour or my expense. We must therefore make that section our *deodand*, or donation to God. Mr Neilson and M. Morne have shown me a second site, more elevated and thus with a larger fall, but with a more friendly geologie, if you may pardon that abstruse term. The old trace and embankments will remain for years as monuments to my folly and the folly of all who fight with the earth.

"We come, in second place, though to it belongs the priority, to the alimentation of the canal through the summer months. I am a woman of grave faults but my enemies are obliged, in the end, to concede that Mme Neilson has ponds. There have been times in my life when I have thought I possessed nothing but ponds. Of that watery endowment, Mr Neilson believes that the Étang des Pâtureaux has the greatest capability of extension."

There was a general turning towards a lieutenant at the back, who beamed like the evening star. Ideas of improvement, even in engineering, rarely come singly. A butt of ridicule, the lad was wonderfully justified.

Mme Neilson picked up her thread. She said: "M. Morne has told me that the pond must be extended by two-and-a-half times. Of course. It must be dammed. Of course. Sluices must be installed and channels dug. But of course. Yet rather than extend its superfice, and thus increase the volume lost each summer to aerial loss or evaporation, it must be deepened. It must be excavated to the greatest depth possible, gentlemen, and certainly to no less than two fathoms, and that will be a hard labour to which I know you are equal."

Mme Neilson halted a moment and looked up from the earth and its secrets. "Yet, all the while that you have dug and delved, the world has not stood still. There are affairs more obstinate than slate and sand, and more grave. I understand from Mr Neilson that the news from America is bad. It is possible, even probable, that next summer you will be called to serve the King in martial, rather than industrial, exercises. Should matters turn out so, which God forbid, these works shall be suspended for a time and possibly for all time."

Mme Neilson paused for a beat, and then a double, and then two more. There was not a sound but the snap of the halyards on the flag-staffs.

"I have therefore decided, after consulting Brigadier Neilson, to offer a bounty of one million francs if the main works are complete to Mr Neilson's satisfaction by the next All Saints' Day coming.

"I would not presume to intermeddle, but it is my wish that a quarter of that sum might pass to the common soldiers."

The officers, who had already spent the whole million in their imaginations, were disappointed, even aggrieved, by Mme Neilson's superfluous and womanly rider. The lady continued: "Come now, gentleman, let us dine and drink a toast to the success of our enterprise."

The tent all but flew away with shouts and flying hats.

There is nothing better than camp food. For a quarter-hour, there was no sound but the champing of military jaws and the glogging of gallant throats. The ladies, even Mlle de Joyeuse, were neglected. The debt to hunger paid, there was a scraping of chairs and a mumbling or roaring of toasts and sentiments, each more foolish than the last, until I thought it wise to call a halt.

Mme Neilson invited me to ride back to La Ferté in her coach. She leaned back against the cushions and closed her eyes.

"May I thank you from my heart, madame?"

"Do not thank me. You may thank, if you wish, Mlle de Joyeuse. The premium was her idea. I was for abandoning the work and paying off the men."

"We shall succeed, madame. I promise."

"Why do you do these things to me? Why, Mr Neilson,

do you set the house on fire so that I must walk in amid the flames to save the furniture?"

"I do not intend it, Jeanne. It is what occurs."

"There will come a time, William, when, whether from my own diminishing strength or the greater force of your adversary, I shall not succeed."

"It is not yet, my lady."

V

As a mark of urgency, and a contribution of force, the Chevalier was excused his after-dinner lesson at the castle, and rose directly from table to ride out to the works. Mme Neilson ruled that he should never leave the side of M. Dalouhe, her master-of-horse and a most steady man. In the way of these things, they were soon separated one from the other, became mere parts of the industrial engine, and I would hear lieutenants shout: "Where is that scamp, Neilson? I must have this carried to H.Q.!" The lad became a favourite of the common soldiers, who ran up a uniform for him, and saluted him with three fingers.

In our absence at the works, M. Duclos, the huntsman, in M. Dalouhe's coat and hat, handed the ladies into the carriage for their after-dinner drive, and took his friend's seat on the box.

On the Sabbath, we dined at the castle. I could see my son wished to startle his sister, his white uniform splashed with mud, his face and neck burned by the sun and the whole contrivance reeking of wood-smoke and the latrine. Mlle de Joyeuse played her part by wrinkling her nose.

"God's bollocks, madame, this tarte is good."

Mme Neilson turned and looked at our son.

Mlle de Joyeuse interposed: "M. le Chevalier, there is no reason to believe the Superintendent of the Universe has human, far less masculine, attributes."

"Mlle de Joyeuse! What is this blasphemous and indecent discourse to do with you!"

"I thought, Maman, you wished me to correct my brother's rare errors of reasoning."

"What is happening to my family? Mr Neilson, can you not instil some discipline in your dependants?"

"Father says 'God's bollocks!'"

"Mr Chevalier, I have used such oaths, but only in military company. I do not wish you to blast the ears of your mother and sister, who are woven of finer stuff than we soldiers are."

The plural personal pronoun enraptured my son, but

also pleased Mme Neilson, and lifted me off the hook. She said:

"M. le Chevalier, I have had excellent reports of your diligence and industry at the works. I would ask that you leave your soldiers' oaths there."

"Yes, my lady."

To remove any colour of favourising, I turned to Mlle de Joyeuse, but she was musing on some island lapped by league after league of blue.

After dinner, my wife and I walked up and down the lime-tree alley, hand-in-hand.

"I grow dull without you, Mr Neilson. Will you not find me a lover from your companions? I prefer gentlemen of the Scottish nation, with black hair and blue eyes."

"Do not say such things, Jeanne, even in jest. You shall wake the Devil from his after-dinner sleep."

"Oh, William, I am sorry." Mme Neilson looked down in confusion. "I should not try to be witty for I have no wit. And, o! I hear the children laughing with you, but when I approach, to share their delight, they stop and look solemn."

"I believe, madame, that in a contented marriage there will be, if you will permit me so barbarous a phrase, a division of labour. You teach our children virtue and religion, and learning and duty and ambition. I show them how to make firecrackers to fright the pious matrons of the convent committee on their visits. Imagine how efficient we would be if I took their catechism and you made magpie-traps. Of their devotion to you, madame, you should not have the smallest doubt."

"Thank you, Mr Neilson. You have, to a degree, reassured me."

VI

That summer of 1754, day turned into night and night into day. The fabric of the regiment disintegrated. It was not that the men became licentious, or any more than general. Rather, they formed into bands under their own leaders, or no leaders at all, and worked by their own laws. Colonel Morne gave orders that food and drink be ready at all hours of day and night.

Beforetimes, when any problem presented itself that might require a deviation from or extension of orders, either M. Morne or I would be consulted. I watched as responsibility slid down the ranks like a squirrel down an oak-bole. Riding at night to the dam at Les Pâtureaux, I came on the Chevalier directing men by torch light. I thought: He shall be a better soldier than I am, because he has studied the profession, rather than practised it, as I have done, *ex tempore.* I never had an idea. What I had was luck, which is not nothing.

We were lying on the clammy bank of the great pond, counting stars.

"May I smoke, sir?"

"On your fourteenth birthday."

"Thank you, Father."

Then, one day like any other, at the outset of September, for no especial reason, and almost simultaneously, we could see the end of our labours. It was as happens sometimes in a dark and tangled wood, when one fancies to see a glimmer ahead; or, after labouring for an hour beside the horses up a steep, one feels through one's boots that the slope is abating.

"Almost there, Brigadier!"

A species of *euphoria* inspired officers and men. The premium shimmered in imagination. That it was now known to have originated with Mlle de Joyeuse superadded the thrill of romance. Each man knew that her eye had fallen on him, and him alone, and only maidenly reticence had caused the gift to be general. More even than that, the sentiment of pride in achieving a difficult labour, which is found in all good soldiers, drove the regiment to prodigies of exertion.

"I shall not hold strictly to the first day of November."

"I believe you should be inflexible, madame. The men are drawn tight as a bow-string. Do not let them relax."

"You know best, dear friend."

VII

When set up beside canalisation, the education of children is a simple affair. As has been related, after the tousle with M. Luynes in the year 1747, the widowed Mme la marquise de Maurepas adopted as her daughter and heiress the foundling from the Hôtel-Dieu of Orléans named Marie-Ange de la Contrition. The child, who was given the name Mlle de Joyeuse, was then nine or ten years of age.

I have said that I was no supporter of the Jacobite cause. None the less, I had business to discharge at the cobweb Stuart Court in exile at Rome, and was away from La Ferté-Joyeuse for the whole summer of that year 'Forty-seven. I was fortunate to keep hold of my life. I was dogged at every step by English spies, imprisoned in the Palace of the Dukes at Venice and attacked on the road by Croate assassins in the service of His Holiness the Pope.

By God's grace, I survived those trials. On my return, I found my lady and I had a son, named William in my recognisance. To legitimate the lad, Mme de Maurepas consented to be my wife. It helped that, at Rome, I had abjured the Protestant cult of my fathers. My wife wrote a new testament, dividing her estate into two parts, god-daughter and son to share-and-share-alike.

Mme Neilson nursed our son herself. That caused some clatter in the district but was seen, on consideration, to be but another instance of Mme Neilson's libertinage, of a piece with her wanton conduct, her chemistry and her industrial adventures. It was as if Mme Neilson were a relic of the Regency of that far-sighted prince, the Duke of Orléans, and quite at angles to the more solid economy and morality of the seventeen-fifties. In the house, it was said that Her Ladyship wished not to burden her posterity with a second surly and immortal pensioner of the character of Mme Plaie, the late duke her father's wet-nurse, still savage in her one hundred and second year. In reality, my wife had long despaired of a child of her body, and saw in the laddie an unmerited gift from God. Nothing she could do for him was sufficient recompense to the Almighty.

My lady herself made his layet, with the assistance of her confidential maid, Mme Dalouhe, and Mlle de Joyeuse. On my return from Italy, I found them cosie at their needles, and it took a times for them to clear a place for me, and to recognise my marital and paternal privileges. It helped that Mme Neilson and I liked each other and my son appreciated the more boist'rous games stocked in my armoury.

In the matter of Mlle de Joyeuse, since neither Mme Neilson nor I would abate a single item of our projects of formation, the foundling was by the age of eighteen proficient in Latin, Greek, Italian, English, mathematics, the piano-et-forte, double-part book-keeping, fine needlework, theology, botany and natural philosophy; and fighting with the short sword and sabre, sharp-shooting, surgery, the bag-pipes, small-boat sailing and infantry tactics. A portion of this knowledge passed, by a species of *friction*, to the Chevalier Neilson, whose childish kingdom began and ended in his adoptive sister. In a very short time, Mme Neilson and I had made our children unmarriageable.

That was put to experiment. In the year 1753, Mme la duchesse de Guise, from the royal house of Lorraine, honoured La Ferté-Joyeuse with a visit. The children staged an entertainment, in which the Chevalier assaulted by escalade a wooden fort, made by the estate carpenters, against a lively defence from Mlle de Joyeuse and the corps of huntsmen. M. Dalouhe had made cartridges of pepper which set the fine company to snuffling and sneezing. At the height of battle, the fort took fire and sprang its powder magazine, which made a good show, and nobody was much hurt. Mme de Guise is a woman of the world, and professed herself ravished by the spectacle, but I sensed some mental reservation in her judgment of our savage millionnaires.

Mlle de Joyeuse seemed to be but half-present. It was as if to attend to her god-parents she required but half a mind.

Veteran soldiers are not always the brightest of lights. I was never no Leibniz, while my breeding, at the High School of Edinburgh, had been broken off at my father's death. I had picked up bits and pieces of knowledge, and some scraps of foreign tongues, in a hail of shot. I own I was not the foundling's mental equal.

Her god-mother, on the other hand, was notorious as the cleverest woman in France. Yet my lady's weaknesses, her pride of purse and pedigree, which as is always the case with the incarnal vices had augmented with the passing years, irritated Mlle de Joyeuse and seemed to diminish in her eyes her benefactress. The girl might have conducted herself with more courtesy had she once heard Mme Neilson say: "When you came from the Hôtel-Dieu of Orléans you possessed a dress and cap worth four and one-half sols. You were marked, with the drabs and assassins, for transportation to Guyane." She knew that Mme Neilson would never speak so.

Where was that other half of her? A part remained with her old duties, for she continued to care for Mme Plaie in the woods. (The alteration was that she carried the evil carline's crock on the pummel of her palfrey and was attended by the hunt-servants *in pleno*.) A portion was devoted to me, as I found one day to my mortification.

"I have engaged for you a man-servant, Mr Neilson."

"Why should I require a man-servant, madame?"

Mme Neilson put down her pen and let her spectacles fall on their ribbon.

"You are no coquet in your dress, Mr Neilson, but you do not precisely adhere to the walls and furniture. Do you know why that is?"

I had not considered the article of my linen.

I said: "Thanks to your kindness, madame, your servants make me half-presentable."

"It is not my servants."

"Oh Lord, do not say . . ."

"No, Mr Neilson. It is not I. Under an arrangement I entered during our troubles, which I regret but cannot abrogate, Mlle de Joyeuse cares for your appearance."

Mme Neilson looked closely at me. "Do you think it is right, Brigadier Neilson, that the future Queen of Benine or Gorée or some other kingdom or principality should have the care of your small clothes?"

"No, I mean, I did not know. If I had known . . ."

"Mr Neilson, you have no conception of cause and effect, only of habitual conjunction. It is a principle more suited to experimental philosophy than household economy."

I managed to defer and then abolish the valet. By a small mercenary contract, I concerted with one of my friends among the laundresses that she wash and press my linen before it were carried to Mlle de Joyeuse.

A part of the girl was engaged with her brother, who never tired or vexed her. I remember when, on his fifth birthday, Mme Neilson first took down his reading-Bible, she found the lad already knew his letters, by the cares of his sister. Her devotion to the Chevalier Neilson was repaid in a love so full and pure it took the breath away.

The office of the lad's gouvernante, filled by Mme Dalouhe, was no more than a charge or sinecure, like the inspectorate of pigs' tongues at the Market Halls of Paris. Mme Dalouhe gave herself up to her teeming family, the consequence of much leisure and a handsome husband. She was rich, touching fifteen hundred francs each year, and all manner of presents, dresses, hats, slippers and unwanted jewels, and stayed in service only for love of her mistress. Confidante, now, in a maternal rather than an illicit passion, she called on Mme Neilson every morning, where her pungent speech supplied some lack or absence in my wife's high occupations; and was often with Mlle de Joyeuse, talking about who knows what.

Mlle de Joyeuse was, it seemed to me, in love. That love was surely returned with all arrearages of interest for there was in the girl no melancholy or agitation, but a sort of lustre, which illumined everything, and made her beautiful beyond description. In the noonday of this love, which was, I suspect, in her estimation, never matched in the history of the world, all else was trivial, vulgar, provisional, clumsy and old-fashioned; or, in the case of the old soldier who had been her first friend, a fanfaronnade from the Comedy. As our love for her became the deeper, so much the more were her god-parents the objects of disdain.

Who was her beloved? It was surely not a neighbour's son, for we made and received few visits. The ladies of the district feared Mme Neilson might address them in Hebrew, or turn them into volatile salts, while my reputation for truculence disheartened their mannies. It was certainly not poor Sergei Pavlovich, the son of my Russian friends, Count and Countess Bielke, as sweet and brave a lad as anyone would wish for son, who had entered His Christian Majesty's service and come with letters from their country place, Deer's Glade in the governorate of Smolensk, in the summer of 'Fifty-three. The laddie suffered for a week until, under the pressing of Mme Neilson, I took what remained of him to tour the fortifications on the Garonne. I wished to say to my god-daughter but did not: "One day, you shall be old and sad and plain like me, and you shall regret your cruelty."

Might it be one of the officers at the canal-excavations? Having made just a single visit, Mlle de Joyeuse had asked to be excused a return, to the great sorrow of her brother. When the lad proposed that Mme Neilson stage a dance for the "fellows at the works", Mlle de Joyeuse showed no enthusiasm and rather the contrary. She did consent to make drawings for the lock-keepers' bothies and very prettie they were, with steep rooves of slate, timber'd walls in *colombe,* as we say, and diamond panes of window-glass.

Was it one of our servants? The old lackeys were scarce a young girl's catch. Was it her saviours in the affair of M. Luynes in 'Forty-seven? Pierre Dalouhe was a man of family, while the hunt-servants were about her always in a body, and would have skinned the man who received from Mlle de Joyeuse so much as a smile. They had erected in her honour a latter-day order of chivalry, yclepit The Order of the Trampled Primrose, after the nosegay of yellow flowers that M. Luynes had offered the lass from horseback to gain her confidence. The fellowship was devoted to the service of the poor, the weak and the fair. In the way of such affairs with young men, the first two objects of the Order, while not wholly neglected, had fallen aside for the promotion of the third.

Jean Duclos, the huntsmen's chief or *primus inter pares*, had commanded the campaign to protect the orphan-girl. During the crisis, Mme Neilson had permitted him to set up head-quarters in her laboratory. The precedent established, he was much to be found there in his off-times, preparing Mme Neilson's experiments or stoking the furnaces.

Many were the complaints of his tyrannical conduct. Since the return of nightingales to La Ferté-Joyeuse in 'Forty-Seven, M. Duclos had reasoned that it would please his mistress more that he multiply the wild creatures on her estate than hobble roebucks for kail-chandlers to wound. Woe betide a tenant who cut his hay before the laverock chicks had fledged, or let his beasts tread down the fritillaries, or grumbled if a lynx took a lamb to share with her darlings. In those assises, Mme Neilson always gave judgment in favour of her tenants, while reserving a word of praise for M. Duclos. It was evident as day that Mme Neilson planned for her chief huntsman some great preferment. M. Ballin's hope of passing his factor's charge to his son looked to me vain. My fear was that M. Duclos' impatient spirit might cause him to leave her service and seek a more extended field for his abilities.

Duclos was exact, while I am a tangle; spoke little, and that to the point, while I rattle; and proud, while I may carouse with beggars and lie in sawdust. I was careful never to give M. Duclos a command.

VIII

For myself, I was occupied in examining tenants for the improved lands on each side of the canal. True to a promise I had made to Mme Neilson, I ensured there were no Protestants admitted or rather that those Protestants that presented themselves were indited as Catholics. January brought rain and February, by God's mercy, two feet of snow. When the water flowed uninterrupted at half a fathom of draught through the summer, I received approaches from public-spirited noblemen and princes who wished for our counsel in schemes of improvement on their own lands. In reality, they wanted me to bear the labour of the works, and Mme Neilson the cost, while they enjoyed the benefice.

I have said that I first came into France from Edinburgh in the year 1720 to serve as a commis or lower clerk in the bank erected at Paris by my townsman, Mr John Law of Lauriston. I spent an evening in the service of that man of genius, and thought myself well instructed in the finances. I had leisure to improve that instruction, for I was judg'd liable for one million livres tournois of the bank's owings and held for six years in the castle of the Bastille at Paris.

I now proposed to my lady that she seek His Christian Majesty's permission to set on foot a general bank at Orléans, with herself as sole shareholder and I as director-general, to lend on mortgage, discount trade bills and make remittances. If Mme Neilson were to deposit cash and good bills to the value of five millions, I would take deposits and issue bank-notes for a further five millions. After the expenses of establishment, the rental of a townhouse, the emoluments of a dozen clerks, porters and guards, and a provision for bad debtors, I believed that Mme Neilson would enjoy a neat profit of 400,000 francs each year.

Mme Neilson debated the scheme over several days. Although that lady cared not at all for what the world had to say of her moral character, of her credit she was jealous to the point of pruderie. She consented to the bank project on three conditions: that the bank-notes be cut into values no smaller than one hundred livres tournois; that she in her own hand sign every note; and that only half of the capital be lent. That last provision would reduce the profit in proportion, and arrest the augmentation of the fund, and for that reason she would forgoe *dividenda* for a period of ten years. When she heard from the secretary of the King's Household that His Majesty required a quarter of the capital as a *don gratuit* or free gift, with another quarter for favoured servants on the same footing, Mme Neilson caulded on the scheme and bade me give it no more of my consideration.

Mme Neilson said: "William, your canal you achieved not simply by reason of your vision and industry, but also because this poor district was *terra incognita* in the eyes of the Court and the Finance. Now that you have, as it were, sketched in La Sologne on the chart of France, you shall need to proceed with circumspection. Or rather, since that is alien to your bold and vigorous nature, I shall do so."

Over the years, Mme Neilson had more than once proposed to buy me the command of the Brigade irlandaise, or Royal Irish. Embodied in His Christian Majesty's service during the Jacobite war in Ireland in the last century, the six regiments fielded excellent men and efficient officers and, by reason of their great steadiness at Fontenoy in 'Forty-five, had earned the gratitude of the maréchal de Saxe and the notice of His Majesty.

I demurred. I believed that, through my incompetence

on Culloden Moor in 'Forty-six, I had killed more than enough Irishmen for any officer in a single lifetime. My company were the best soldiers I ever directed, if only for a night and a day. Only they stood their ground after the Highland men had left the field and our regulars put down their arms. Without so much as forming square, they scattered a troop of English horse, poor Captain Chumley's. Not a day passed but that they did come before my eyes and rebuke me.

Also, except in the matter of my recovery from the Isle of Barray after the battle on the moor – an affair of some quarter-million francs – it was my settled principle never to accept from my wife riches or honours or anything but the pleasure of her company and the lights of her mind. I found myself, on half-pay, but one of dozens of dead-wood officers whose exploits in the King's service had long ago been forgotten or obscured by the glories of younger men. To compound my redundancy, I had never commanded regular men on the continent of Europe. My fights were all of a muddle. Gingee we had taken by storm; Astarabad by stealth; and HMS *Galatea* by stratagem. I had fought but one pitched battle in Europe, that at Culloden, and killed my whole force.

IX

The visit of our English friends, Mr and Mrs Harris, which occurred in the summer of 'Fifty-five, was not at first easy. After the fight on Culloden Moor, poor Mr Harris had been under a cloud. It was said that, during that action, he had displeased H.R.H. the Duke of Cumberland, the King of Great Britain's younger son and commander of the Royal army. It helped Mr Harris not at all that in Scotland he was said to have refused the order to give no quarter for the rebels and even (it was whispered) to have spirited away to the western islands a wounded Jack officer. Scottish opinion was at that time of small price, and even of some cost. In his letters, Mr Harris spoke of selling up. Since Mme Neilson now had much property in Great Britain, that lady proposed engaging him as her English man of business. That, like everything else, had to wait on the peace.

Yet it is war that sets Fortune at play. At the fall of Bergen-op-Zoom in the late war, Mr Harris not only held off the French assault in the market place but, after night had fallen, brought the remanent of his company to safety. He was gazetted Colonel and presented to King George at his levy. His Majesty asked for an account of the fight and gave Harris a thousand pounds. The smile of the father trumped the sneer of the son, who was (it was said) well enough for hanging bare-arsed Scotchmen but no adversary for the maréchal de Saxe. None the less, it would not do to speak of the battle by Culloden House. I was not sure that even Mme Harris knew what had occurred. When I conveyed that, with as much tact as I possessed, to Mme Neilson, she nodded and returned to her letters.

Mme Neilson made a great friend of Harris. Mrs Harris, in contrast, though pretty and gay, spoke no words of French and had no philosophical interests. She had carried with her from across the Channel fixed ideas of the superiority of English manners, dress, government, cookery and manufactures over their French congeners. It is possible, besides, that Mme Neilson did not show herself at her sweetest with other ladies. It would have been better had the Harrises brought their children.

Mlle de Joyeuse retrieved the visit. She spoke English with more ease than her god-parents, and decided for reasons only she knew to make all well. She had M. Dalouhe harness the state coach, which weighed two ton and required three pairs of horses. The great earth shook as the young ladies drove out, dressed to the nines, Mrs Harris in the seat facing forward, the Joyeuse blazon on the doors and four running footmen. At the sight of the *juggernaute*, our neighbours came to their bottom steps, dug out some words of English or, if they were bold, inquired of Milady Harris for news of those quarrelsome nations, the Wigths and the Torries. The young ladies returned in gusts of laughter. The Chevalier and M. Duclos took Harris wildfowling.

"Such a strange thing, Brigadier Neilson," Mrs Harris whispered at supper. "Harris tells me your 'keeper speaks English."

Damnation!

"Mr Duclos is not my gamekeeper, Mrs Harris, but Mme Neilson's. You would much oblige me if," and here I took her arm, "you would treat that as a secret between us. Mr Duclos is a good man and I would not wish him thought presomptuous."

Mrs Harris winked an eye. "Mum's the word."

She did not keep it, but was for ever saying, when we met a crux in translation: "Should we not enquire from our woodland savant, Mr Neilson?"

By good luck, and bad habit, Mme Neilson was not listening.

Mrs Harris proposed that Mlle de Joyeuse return with her to London. In that city, the lass might enjoy the opera theatre, would attend the Drawing-Room at the palace of Saint-James and be presented to the Dowager Princess of Wales. I suspected that such a charming and accomplished *protégée* (as we say in France) would do no harm to Mrs Harris' own standing at the English Court. Thence Mlle de Joyeuse would go to live with Mrs Clerk of Auldbiggin in the Lawnmarket of Edinburgh, who was my near relation, and carry Mme Neilson's good wishes to Dr Black and Dr Cullen and her other philosophical correspondents in that learned city. The fond god-parents raised no objection, but Mlle de Joyeuse begged not to be separated from her maman. Mrs Harris assured us that Mme Neilson might live at London and in North Britain in incognito, as an aunt or somesuch, but Mlle de Joyeuse raised so many cavills that the plan fell away.

It being warm, we supped each night on the terrace. After supper, Harris and I drew our chairs away so we might smoke our pipes, and young William joined the combusting party. Coats and ties slid into darkness.

Harris was thoughtful. At length, he said: "When I think of the fight at the temple . . ."

"My son, Mr Harris took me prisoner in India in 'Forty-five."

"Took my father prisoner!"

"Your father, Mr Chevalier, had fallen into an unsavoury pond and was beset by magars—"

"Crocodiles."

"Oh!"

"When I think, I say, of that day in India and this evening," and here Harris took a deep inhalation and surveyed the darkling scene, "and all about us starlight and fair ladies, and a young soldier of the greatest promise, and the vasty fields of France . . ."

Mr Harris fell silent.

"What?"

"What?"

"I have said enough. To say more would be to tempt Fate."

My son was at a loss.

"Colonel Harris means, young man, that we, he and I, are the most fortunate men who ever lived and would do well to say our thanks to God."

"Oh!"

X

How much soever that we love our guests, their departure is never entirely mournful. Mme Neilson returned to her letters and air pumps, and my children and I to tennis and horse-races.

The peace was short-lived.

It was not my habit to disturb Mme Neilson in the

mornings, but that post-day I did so. The lady looked up with an expression of interest at the disturbance to the legal order.

I said: "I have received an Italian letter from il signor marchese di Gabiano, who is one of the principal bankers at Genoa. It concerns Mlle de Joyeuse."

"Are you acquainted with Signor Gabiano, Mr Neilson?"

"Not at all. I doubt that my friend M. Blondeau at Venice may be the introductor."

A merchant of varied commerce, M. Blondeau had befriended me at a time of peril in that city, and also sold Mme Neilson a great many sacred pictures. For Mlle de Joyeuse on her fifteenth birthday, he had sent a superb cembalo. M. Blondeau knew more about my family than I knew.

"Go on, if you please, sir."

"The Duke of Modena is indebted to the Genoese bankers."

"I know that, William."

"Mme Jeanne, I tell you this not because I approve of it but so that I should keep nothing from you."

"I am glad of that. Please continue."

"Signor Gabiano wonders if a match between the young Prince of Modena and Mlle de Joyeuse might not be of advantage to both houses."

"Though not as richly as to the advantage of the house of Gabiano since Mlle de Joyeuse's dowry will be attached to discharge His Royal Highness' debts."

"I had not thought of that."

"Really, Mr Neilson! Because you yourself are spotless in your conduct of money matters, you assume too readily that others are so."

"I believe that Mlle de Joyeuse should be consulted. The Este are an old family—"

"Semi-old," Mme Neilson said.

". . . and perhaps have not the vigour they once possessed. The young prince has been much unwell. What if they do not like?"

Mme Neilson looked away. "Once Mlle de Joyeuse has borne an heir to the House of Modena, I imagine she may please herself."

"I did not know you were so worldly, madame."

Mme Neilson blushed. "It is not I that am worldly, Mr Neilson. It is that you are absolutely unworldly. Mlle de Joyeuse is right. You are still the youth striding with bright eyes through the Caledonian heather."

She recovered herself. "Our son will follow you into the King's service, but Mlle de Joyeuse shall have a throne. I tell you that, William, so that you know."

"And why must she have a throne, madame?"

"To show the world that God is just."

"It is your accursed family ambition!"

Mme Neilson flared up and just as soon cooled down. She said: "Shall we not take a turn, Mr Neilson, in our garden?"

I forgot to say that, back in 'Forty-seven, my lady and I had fought such a fight that I had damaged part of her bed-chamber. Mme Neilson proposed that famous night that, when we felt a quarrel coming on, we should execute it *in the fresh*, as the Italians say. As it turned out, we had lived near ten year in perfect happiness and harmony, and had made no use of that extra-mural resort.

Our children were schooling a horse on the terrace, the Chevalier up, Mlle de Joyeuse at the lunging rein. The lass looked at us with that half-interest of hers.

"Are you going for a quarrel?"

Mme Neilson halted. She said: "As a matter of fact, young lady, we are. And your carping tongue does not improve our tempers."

"Have a care of my young trees, Brigadier."

The consequence was that, though both Mme Neilson and I were boiling with rage, it was not rage at each other. We were like mortal enemies awash in a high sea, clinging to the same spar. Whether by intention or malice, Marie-Ange de la Contrition de Joyeuse had slain our quarrel.

"It is not family pride, dear friend. Mlle de Joyeuse is a young person who can do great good in the world. You yourself said, in a phrase that surprised me at the time, that the first woman is of greater use than the last man. I took that to mean that in the incidence of hazard or probability, the first woman, who comes from a popular of millions, will be of greater worth than the last man, from a popular of one."

"My reasoning was not so statistical, my lady."

"William! Italy will not for ever be a carpet on which foreign powers to play at soldiers, or a butcher's table to serve Courts with nothing better to do but carve up a fair land. One house will unite the peninsula, send Austria and Spain running, wake Venice from her watery slumber, scruff Genoa from her moidores and cruzados, retrench the temporal encroachments of His Holiness. Who knows if that will not be the Este? *Rimasa come sanza vita, aspetta qual possa esser quello che sani le sue ferite.* Such that, abandoned as if lifeless, Italy waits for the one that shall heal her wounds . . . But you have read Signor Machiavelli?"

"In prison, my lady. You may recollect that, after the bankruptcy of Mr Law's bank at Paris, though but a second clerk, I was held indebted to the King for the sum of one million francs. I was in the Bastille of Saint-Antoine for six years."

Mme Neilson looked at me as if her thought had made an unexpected *détour*.

"Did you have many books in the Castle of the Bastille?"

"I had a Mayence bible, the Milan *editio princeps* of Horace and Machiavelli's *Discourses on Livy* printed by Aldus at Venice. Whoever sent them saved my poor life."

"Not the Homer?"

"No, my lady."

"I was ordered never again to write to you."

"I am sorry."

"I was not punished for sending you my father's books, Mr Neilson. I was married to M. de Maurepas."

"O Jeannette! What did I do to you! I wrecked your life and happiness."

Mme Neilson looked away. "Whatever I did, I did of my own will, and I wish it had been more." She said, so quietly I scarcely heard it: "You received, at least, the money I sent to Milord de Bigby? I obeyed my father's command in the letter rather than in the intention."

In the prison, Puss used to bring me sparrows and starlings, the which I roasted on a stick. One morning, she caught a pair of young pigeons, and on another, a song-thrush, which I would say was the best eating.

"Mr Neilson, would you kindly answer?"

Once, Puss bustled in with a chicken-bone from the guard-room. I remember craunching it to liquid in my teeth. Now I understood how Mr Bigby feasted his little men. It was Jeanne's money intended for me. And o! My letter to my mother in Scotland, Mr Bigby never sent it!

"Forgive me, madame. I fell into day-dream. I did not receive money from Mr Bigby as such, but I had hospitality from him. He kept an open table for those guests of the King less fortunate than he was."

"So you did not starve. Thank God."

"I did not starve. Thank God."

XI

In marriage, the jutting or prominent edges of the character are worn away. In observing myself through the eyes of an uninformed spectator, I could see that I was a more polished article than the lad who escaladed the wall of the Banque Royale at Paris in the month of December of 1720. I was neater in my dress, more courteous in speech, more careful in action. Mme Neilson, rubbing each day against me and her children, had become less impatient of the dull and foolish; less strict in her religious observances; less sombre in her manners.

What had abated not a jot was her pride. Mme Neilson was proud of her scientific and philosophical discoveries. She was proud of having made good the late duke her father's pillages and restored the Joyeuse name and estate for her posterity. She was proud of her thousand-year pedigree and wished it preserved for another thousand years.

She herself was wed to a penniless Scotsman under sentence of death in his home-country, but that was but an exception or limiting case to a marital rule established over more than fifty contracts of marriage, always with knightly families distinguished in war or the King's service, or retired amid their people on their lands; some of those families of great estate and some of mediocre; but all of the names of Rohan, Guesclin, Guise, Harcourt, Rabutin, La Rochefoucauld. In the cases of Mlle de Joyeuse and the Chevalier, that rule would be enforced as if nothing had occurred in the interval.

If those sentiments be deemed sinful, or at best worldly, they are explained (if not excused) by a tint of the eternal.

The house of Joyeuse, to which I was allied by law and affection, possessed a secret. The secret lay in a small vaulted room without window below the chapel in the north-eastern angle of the castle. The secret was known to three living persons: Mme Neilson, Mlle de Joyeuse and this author.

On an oak board in the room, lit day and night by two candles in iron holders, there rested a glass dish, smashed and repaired and bound by wires of gold. It seemed to absorb devotion as it absorbed the light. Retrieved from the Holy Land by Hugues de Joyeuse on the First Crusade, its survival was entrusted to each generation of the Joyeuse family for such time as that generation lived on earth. It was the family's blazon, repeated on every banner, coach-door, boss and bed-sheet, and on the handkerchief sewed into my shirt, the Joyeuse talisman and burden: *Sable, ane chalice argent.* Mme Neilson had not inherited the Saint Grail. It had inherited Mme Neilson, and would in time inherit the foundling and the Chevalier. I was the penitent knight, dozing over his weapons before the door, dead to the world.

"If you will permit me to interrupt your reverie, Mr Neilson, I have a question for you."

We were promenading in Mme Neilson's garden.

"I shall answer."

"Why do you call me Jeannette?"

"It was the name of my mother, madame. Except that in Scotland, the name is spelled J-O-N-E-T."

"I wonder, sometimes, how you can suffer me, Mr Neilson, for I believe I am insufferable. I am honoured to have the name of the lady who brought you into the world.

Please call me Jeannette, whenever and wherever you wish it."

"You do not speak of your own mother."

"I never knew her in the world, as it were. She died at my birth."

"Ah!"

"And what does 'Ah!' signify, Mr Neilson?"

"Nothing at all, madame. It is a Scottish interjection of distress and fellow-feeling."

"You are not being clever, are you, Mr Neilson? I do not like cleverness in men."

"With justice, madame."

"If by your horrid and impertinent 'Ah!', you mean that I saw in Mlle de Joyeuse an image of myself as an orphan child, you are quite wrong. Such a thought never for a moment crossed my mind."

"I am sure, my lady."

"Now kindly leave me, Mr Neilson. Be so good as to write to M. Gabiano and say that the Court of Modena must deal with Mme Neilson directly and not through merchant-bankers at Genoa. You may add, as from yourself, that H.R.H.'s plenipotentiary must hold at least the rank of ambassador."

XII

The Count of Provarma was an old soldier who had fought like a lion under Saxe, then fawned his way into the Duke of Modena's confidence, and lived at ease on gossip and women. We were instructed by Mme Neilson aforetimes to be ignorant of Italian. Il signor Provarma spoke French to perfection, and so there was no advantage. At supper the first evening of the visit, Mlle de Joyeuse made a brief discourse on the theme of Christian virtue. The Chevalier's ears were on stalks. It was clear to me that the girl had something up her sleeve. After supper, Mlle de Joyeuse played a bagpipes sonata of her own composition, the Chevalier furnishing continuo on the bassoon. M. Provarma applauded.

After my lady and children had retired, M. Provarma and I drank a dozen of Burgundy, but since we both had hollow legs and soldiers' heads, we called Pax at the foot of the twelfth. I wished to act honourably by Mme Neilson. I insisted that the Princess of Modena must have her own court and servants, maintained out of her dowry, and a say in the naming of ministers. Beyond the dowry, her husband would have no rights over her fortune and succession. M. Provarma made a glancing remark about her orphandom. I wondered aloud if the

King of France would permit so great a property to leave his kingdom. Light was beginning to slink through the curtains and, amid dead men and dying candles, we called it a night, having advanced the project not one step.

I called on my lady, who woke up.

"I hope you are not feeling affectionate. Your breath, Mr Neilson, would cause a circumlunar eclipse."

"I shall exercise temperance. Do you wish to hear of the negociation?"

"Can you not do both at once?"

"No, madame."

"Oh! I can. Well, let us manage the two affairs, as we say in Latin, *seriatim.* You may carefully take up my chemise and, if you wish, kiss me."

"Now, to the other business."

"M. Provarma demands as Mlle de Joyeuse's dowry four million piastres at Genoa and, as his pot of wine, one hundred thousand scudi at Rome—"

"What impudence! Refused."

". . . an half-share in the canal—"

"Refused."

". . . and a husband's right over the Princess' succession."

"Refused."

Mme Neilson yawned. "For all your carousal, dear friend, you do not seem to have advanced very far."

"No, my lady."

"Your strength is in war and love, not diplomacy and the doings of Courts."

"Ours is an epoch of distinct trades, madame."

"Life with you, Mr Neilson, is all tops-and-turvey, but not without its glories. By reason of your Bacchic kisses, I shall be drunk at Mass, as well as in a state of sin. Will you not leave me so I can make some repairs to my conscience?"

"A parting kiss?"

"Yes, all right, if you like."

XIII

I was sure that Mlle de Joyeuse intended to do M. Provarma a bad turn: in the saddle, in the tennis-court or in the exercise-hall. Nothing of the sort happened.

Riding out into the woods, we proceeded at a walk. Mlle de Joyeuse questioned M. Provarma about the vulgar tongue of Italy and its descent from Latin, but not so deeply as to exhaust his small philology.

In the tennis-play, I thought it best to have them on

the same side of the net. That rebounded on me. The Chevalier, a player of talent but a wild one, hit M. Provarma three times. The poor man must have thought he was back in the wood at Fontenoy.

Because of our wounds, and the listening walls of the castle, we made our negociation in the open air. On those head-to-head strolls, I tried to divert Count Provarma always to the eastern or mechanical of the two wings or, as they are called, commons, but his curiosity was like that of an unschooled spaniel. I was showing him the kitchen-step where, on April 28th, 1429, on the march to relieve the city of Orléans from the English, Jeanne d'Arc had begged a cup of water. From the exercise-hall on the western side, we heard Mlle de Joyeuse calling out points.

"I believe I might test a blade against the young princess."

"We must ask Mme Neilson's permission."

"Of course. Mme Neilson. Her permission," M. Provarma said.

That was discourteous, but I let it go by. Not so Mlle de Joyeuse, who was standing in the door of the exercise-hall.

"With your blessing, Brigadier, I should like to have instruction. I have much to learn of the Italian school of fencing."

I was not in the habit of refusing anything to Mlle de

Joyeuse. M. Provarma walked to the armory and selected a weapon.

I called: "*Mettez-vous en garde!*"

Take your stand!

Mlle de Joyeuse fought in a defensive posture. What startled me, and caused the Chevalier to gape, was her poor movement. What made her such a swordswoman, surely the best in Europe and better than all but a few men, was her balance, which more than preponderated her lesser strength. If ever the Chevalier had, by maladroitness, pricked her, she would have bled ichor.

"Heels, mademoiselle! Heels in line!"

Devil your conceit, you pop-headed Italian!

Whenever a woman succeeds in a man's pursuit, she adds phantasy, turns pride into grace. M. Provarma could not seek to land a point without appearing a bully. Yet the schemer in him wanted to frighten the princess, and the man to master the woman.

M. Provarma made his Sunday strike. His foil flew from his hand, hung a moment in the air, fell and splintered on the pavement. He was open on four quarters but Mlle de Joyeuse raised her weapon.

"*Dégagez-vouz!*"

Separate!

I feared young William would cry out, "Sis, why didn't

ye stick 'im?" He did not. My son was learning, in pain. His beloved friend had become an item of property.

I handed M. Provarma a second foil and right gauntlet.

"Mettez-vous en garde!"

Provarma now saw how far he was overmatched. To end without score might be gallant, but to be pricked by a young girl would destroy him not just in his self-esteem but in what he assumed (incorrectly) to be our estimate of him. It is possible, also, that he had come to recognise that everything he had thought about Mlle de Joyeuse and the Modena match was illusion. A mere girl, she had seen into his deceitful heart. Far from making his fortune at the Court of Modena, she might ruin him whenever and wherever she deigned. The bout proceeded with all the dash of a Latin sermon. To cheer M. Provarma, I offered to do three sets and we near killed each other.

XIV

The next morning I was summoned to attend Mme Neilson. She was, as always at that time of day, seated at her writing desk. Once the door had closed behind me, Mme Neilson looked up and smiled, most sinisterly.

"Mr Neilson: at what annual rent or rate of interest does His Royal Highness of Modena receive his funds?"

"Ten per cent and rising."

"At what rate do I borrow?"

"The canal loans were struck at 2 per cent, on the security of your jewels."

"So, with my caution and guarantee, His Royal Highness' bankers will receive, on a 2 per cent risk, an annual rent not of 2 per cent but of 10 per cent?"

"Yes, my lady."

"If that is so, Mr Neilson, shall the Genoese gentlemen wish to lend more to His Royal Highness or less?"

"More, my lady."

"Will they urge him to build palaces and plaisances and to keep a lavish table and equipage? Will they show him jewels for his mistresses?"

"All those things, my lady."

"And will that help or hinder the young Princess of Modena?"

"Hinder, my lady."

"So, dear Mr Neilson, you must find a way to limit His Royal Highness' borrowing."

"It appears so, Socrates."

Mme Neilson looked at me. "Are you teasing me, Mr Neilson?"

"God forbid!"

Mme Neilson was flustered. "Actually, the ironic or Socratic style in argument, though irritating to the weaker disputant, is a capital way of establishing the truth."

"So I have heard."

I was taking my leave when she said, pianissimo: "Shall you write to the Stuart Court at Rome?"

"What did you say, Mme Neilson?"

I must have been terrible to behold.

"Repeat what you said, madame."

"I knew when I married you that you would give me orders, and so it is."

"I am not ordering, but asking. Are you contemplating, madame, consigning Mlle de Joyeuse to the ruined and exiled Stuart Court, and uniting her to a Prince of Wales who has lost all hope of life?"

"Mr Neilson, you have no policy. It is an amiable characteristic, but in this matter it is an obstacle. I did not for an instant contemplate a match between Mlle de Joyeuse and Charles Stuart, Prince of Wales. Had you written as I asked, the English postal spies would have opened your letter, and brought the weight of the English ministry to bear on Modena. Or themselves offered a more brilliant candidate for Mlle de Joyeuse's hand and dowry."

Mme Neilson turned aside her head. "Also, Mr Neilson, I do not especially cherish being wedded to a proscript."

"You never mentioned that before. In all our years together . . ."

"I did not wish to burden you. Yet it is so. My preference is not important but what if, by the fortunes of war or sea, you found yourself on English ground and subject to English law? I am told that to be hanged is not so great a disgrace in England as it is in France, but did you wish to widow me on Tibourne Hill? And orphan your son like his sister? Had you permitted me to proceed, I would have demanded from King George, as the price of annulling the Stuart match, your free pardon."

Mme Neilson had a gift for creating facts of long, even permanent, establishment. I wished, not for the first time, that I had been matriculated at the College of Edinburgh and read the whole class of Rhetoric so as not always to be bested in argument by Mme Neilson.

"Do as you please, madame. I shall take my leave."

"As you wish. The matter is closed and shall never be re-opened. Your honour is precious to me."

"I have none." It was time to tell the truth. "My lady, when I was in Italy in 'Forty-seven, King James asked me to carry a second army into Scotland."

"I know."

"I accepted command of the force."

"I know."

"I betrayed you."

"You wished to be true to your Irish men, cruelly done to death on the Moor."

"Will you forgive me?"

"There is nothing to forgive."

XV

I cast up Mme Neilson's order into legal gibberish, and presented it to Count Provarma. He read it in snorts, like a horse being washed in a farm pond.

I said: "Mme Neilson will guarantee His Royal Highness' bills but on the inflexible condition that each is endorsed in the hand of the Princess of Modena. The contract shall be printed, at Mme Neilson's expense, at Genoa, Venice, Geneva, Lyon and Paris."

"It is a disgraceful demand. The Court will not agree to it, for I shall not convey it."

"So be it. Do not for a moment think that Mlle de Joyeuse has no other suitors. Mlle de Joyeuse is an accomplished young person. In a commonwealth or republic . . ."

M. Provarma shuddered.

". . . she might have risen on her merits to the highest offices of state."

"You are opposed to this match, are you not, Mr Neilson?"

"My opinion is of no consequence. There is only one authority in this house, and that is Mme Neilson. I tender advice in matters of hydraulic architecture, where I am expert."

"For God's sake, man, how can you take orders from a woman!"

"Because, M. Provarma, it is better to obey a sensible woman than a foolish man."

"Damn you! That is discourteous to my master! I shall have satisfaction!"

"I was precisely as discourteous to your master as you were to my mistress. I react to breaches of truce always at the same calibre, never heavier, never lighter. If you wish to fight me, M. Provarma, I am at your service. Howsoever the fight turns out, it is the end of this negociation and, I suspect, your residence at the Court of Modena. You would do well to take my pleasanterie in good part."

The contino di Provarma made a display of laughing. He slapped me on the shoulder and said: "What a fine fellow you are!"

XVI

That was the end of it.

Mme Neilson said: "M. Provarma took his leave of me this morning. He did not seem to be in the best of tempers. What have you done to the poor man, Mr Neilson?"

"His Royal Highness has his six millions, but at the price of servitude to a young girl who will slice him in two if he crosses her. It is not an ideal arrangement." I had a sudden fear for the lass. "Do they still poison in Italy?"

"As far as I am aware, the Este have developed no special aptitude for poisoning. I know you shall yourself overlook Her Royal Highness's protection."

"Naturally."

I began to sing:

"*Bevilo bianco bevilo nero bevilo pure come vuoi tu.*"

Drink the white wine or the red, or however you would like it.

"Mr Neilson, your levity is sometimes wearying."

"May I take my leave?"

That was also Mme Neilson's wish. As I left, I hummed as to myself:

"*Cos'è sto vino così giallino? Sarà l'avanza di ieri ser.*"

How is this wine so yellow in colour?

It must be left over from last night.

XVII

Since the passage of arms between his sister and M. Provarma, my son had become sullen. One morning, to my surprise, he sought me out alone.

"May we speak in French, Father?"

"Of course."

"It concerns Mlle de Joyeuse."

"Do you have your sister's permission to speak to me?"

Young William looked downcast. "No, sir."

I said: "My son, let us perform an experiment. Imagine your sister is sitting, here, beside me, with her head laid on my shoulder, as she sometimes likes to do. Say your piece, but look not at me, but at the image or simulacrum of your sister."

The lad took a breath. "You may know, sir, that Mlle de Joyeuse was not born to great estate."

"*Nescias an te generum beati,* and so on."

"Yes, sir. I myself am certain Mlle de Joyeuse is at least of royal stock. None the less, Father, you may not know but she was once a servant in this house."

"Look at your sister not at me, sir!"

The lad gave up.

I said: "Are you saying, my son, that Mlle de Joyeuse would prefer for husband a man of worth whatever his birth or station?"

Young William turned away.

"Come, dear boy," I said. "Let me embrace you." He was all bones in my arms. I continued: "M. Dalouhe has found a pair of trench mortars in the commons. He believes they were cast during the Fronde."

The lad burst from my arms. "We shall dig zic zac entrenchments. And pound La Ferté to powder."

"Hold your horses, lad. M. Fougue must test that the metal of the barrels and casings is sound. And we must consult your mother. She may wish for part of her house to be preserved."

There the matter rested, in a tattoo of running slippers and slammed doors.

XVIII

Until the year 1756, when we got again into a war with England. I received a note from Mr Harris saying that he was ordered back to India, where we had begun our friendship, and hoped that I might request some other theatre of action lest he be obliged to take me prisoner a second time. In truth, I was weary of the King's service, but not so weary that I did not wait with drawn breath for the post.

The arpentage of the canal lands no longer occupied

me. Each side of the canal, I had made, or improved, twelve thousand English acres of cultivable land, and nearly twice that of prairie or good pasture. A portion of the corn was to be left in the ear so as to entertain, on their visits in autumn, a clan of grue or crane-birds, to which Mme Neilson was devoted. Her ordinance, enforced with unpardonable rigour by Duclos, was much resented.

I had laid out five villages in a plain, military architecture, and built four stone barns, two grain-mills and a bone-mill, and three churches (in the style of Saint Anne's at Calcutta). I had dug twenty-three locks, each with its lock-keeper's bothy and garden, and made on the embankments on one side a haulage-path for horses and a foot-way on the other. I had excavated basins at each end of the canal and at the half-way station so that boats could load and unload without impeding one another. I had surveyed, ditched and surfaced forty miles of roads, with a causey of twenty feet broad so two carts and a rider might pass at the same moment without entanglement. Twenty feet back on each side, I had planted poplar-trees, to shade the weary foot-passenger and dusty cavalier. I had built twenty-four cart bridges and two aqueducts or *ponts-canaux*.

I was as restive as an old war-horse.

"Must you pace so, Mr Neilson?"

"Am I pacing, madame?"

"I believe you are. Like a lawyer without a brief at the Palais de Justice of Paris."

Mme Neilson took off her spectacles. "Am I become Omphale, obliging Hercules to carry a distaff and spin wool? Or Thetis, hiding Achilles among the daughters of Skyros? What I fear beyond all is that some Ulysses will come here and trick you so that you pick up a sword."

XIX

Sometimes, when I was without occupation, or in the dumps, I turned my steps to the room I first occupied at the castle, at the top of a spirale stair in the south-eastern turret. I was told that I was brought there on the last day of 1746, carried up the steps by M. Dalouhe and laid out in a cot that had served in the past for the repose of visiting lackeys. I had been wounded in the battle on Culloden Moor and spirited off the field; dragged here and there through secret places in the highlands and islands; and carried over to France by M. Douvry, the Dunkirk privateer. It was in that little room, with its view from a slit window over the kitchens and bakehouse, moat and commons, that I made my convalessence. It was there that Mlle de Joyeuse, in the time she was a barefoot kitchen-maid, tended me. It was there that M. Duclos and I plotted the confounding of the comte de Luynes.

Duclos had a way of appearing without having made a sound. I would look round and he would be in the door-frame, neither my servant nor my friend, but with his purpose united, for a time, to mine.

Ah, was there ever on earth such a fool as you, William Neilson?

Duclos had loved the foundling even before he saved her life, perhaps since the inoculation against the small-pox, perhaps even before. He had loved Mlle de Joyeuse when she was a dirty kitchen jurr. It was not his fault that she had become a millionnairess. He had fought his love or sought, in the Order of the Trampled Primrose, to make it multiple and ridiculous. It was not his fault that she loved him.

I heard the swish of skirts and, turning, saw not god-mother but god-daughter. Mlle de Joyeuse started, and then sat down beside me on the bed.

I said: "I come to remember our times together."

"Likewise."

"Oh lass, we were such friends."

"I am your friend if you are mine." The bars were up again.

"Do you wish me to speak to your maman about M. Duclos?"

"No, sir! No!"

"Should you not tell your maman that you prefer him?"

"No."

"Why not?"

"Because Maman shall dismiss him. Or worse."

"Are you sure? Mme Neilson knows his worth, as do I."

"Maman wants me to be Princess of Modena."

"Please, my darling, will you let me explain? In the vacancy in the île de France, that is, after the death of M. de Maurepas in 'Thirty-Two, and before the arrival of M. de La Bourdonnais in 'Thirty-Five, your maman governed the island with wisdome and success. Those three years were for her the most useful, and therefore the happiest, time in her life. She wishes something of the same for you."

"At Modena?"

"That is not worthy of you, mademoiselle."

The lass flounced away and then returned.

"Do you swear that you will not tell Maman?"

"I do not swear, for I am told I am too given to swearing and swearing is not here necessary. We are going to your maman now, and you shall tell her."

Mlle de Joyeuse stood stock-still, and then nodded.

"Brave Marie-Ange de la Contrition," I said.

XX

I had long known that Mlle de Joyeuse, once she had decided on a course of action, did not hesitate or deflect. Mme Neilson's apartment lay at the end of an enfilade of rooms, each longer and richer than its precedent. As Mlle de Joyeuse progressed, she looked neither to one or t'other side, head erect, back straight, like the emissary of a distant and huffy empire.

We found Mme Neilson in tears, rocking back and forth. Mlle de Joyeuse flew at her.

"Oh Maman, do not weep!"

Mme Neilson stood up. She had a letter in her hand.

"I am not weeping, dearest. I am happy." She smiled so that her eyes sparkled. "Our friend, Mr Neilson, is to have at last his general's badge." She held out the letter but let it fall and I caught it in the air.

"Before I read this letter, Mlle de Joyeuse has something to say."

"Can it wait, puppet?"

"Yes, Maman."

The letter was from M. le marquis de Montcalm, dated from Québec, in Canada, November 15th of the past year.

Dear cousin,

It is with reluctance that I write to you, madame. I have put off writing, in the hope that our fortunes here might turn, but the ice is coming down the river, and unless the vessel L'Abénakise *puts out sail today, she may be beset. I, too, am beset not just by the hazards of war in a wild country – though those are hard enough – but by the incompetence of the King's servants and the treason of the King's munitioners who bleed this poor colony dry.*

I must have your husband by me, madame, else I am lost and Canada with me and our beautiful France. There is no officer in Europe more capable than M. Neilson in the direction of native auxiliaries, more trustworthy, more imaginative and with greater experience. My officers are of the same opinion as is M. le marquis de Vaudreuil, the Governor General. You will find here-enclosed M. Neilson's Camp-Marshal's brevet, signed by me on His Majesty's behalf. His appointments are 25,000 livres a year and a 10,000-franc gratification at departure, payable at Paris.

The bitter winter is upon us. For seven months, I shall have no word from you and I shall be in an agony. Yet in my heart, I know that you shall let General Neilson go, and he shall come safe across the water, and we shall prevail.

I am, madame, your most obedient servant,
Montcalm
P.S. Do you remember stealing peaches at Candiac?

I said: "I would wish to have the affair of Modena broken off before I leave for New France."

"You are leaving, husband?"

"Would you have me deaf to a brother officer's appeal? How could I look my son in the eye? Or Mlle de Joyeuse? Or you, the love of my life?"

"You know about the pitcher and the well."

"Even so."

Mlle de Joyeuse spoke. She said: "Your son needs you, General. Canada is lost. You said that yourself."

"Even so, my darling. The Chevalier shall come to me at fourteen years of age. Until that time, I request that there be no advance in the treaty with the Court of Modena and that it is for Mlle de Joyeuse to express her preference."

Mme Neilson stood up. She said: "Mlle de Joyeuse, will you be so kind as to wake the Chevalier and bring him to the small chapel where he shall find us? He need not dress. There, we shall ask God's blessing on General Neilson's campaign."

So we knelt, confused by sleep, grief, fear and regret,

before a smashed and restituted glass dish which we believed, in varying degree, and all hoped, to be the Holy Grail. Some special blessing had preserved me in the riot of my life and that was surely not my wit nor my right arm. I carried with me at all times its worn image on the handkerchief Jeanne had given me at our first meeting at the Bank in Paris: *Sable, ane chalice argent.* As I rode out, I felt the cloth against my heart.

XXI

I had hoped to make the traverse with the recruits and victuals in the munitioner's fleet from Bordeaux, but was held up at Court. The King was most gracious, and inquired after Mme Neilson and our children. He asked me to exert myself in Canada to the utmost to abate the cruel conduct of our native allies. I promised to do so. His Majesty appeared better instructed in Canadian affairs than his servants.

At the Department of Marine, I learned that at the capture in the year just passed of Fort Guillaume-Henry, at the southern end of the lac du Saint-Sacrement, M. Montcalm had lost command of the native men who had killed and scalped the English wounded and prisoners to the number of some two hundred. But for the intervention of one of the chiefs, M. Montcalm would have suffered the same bloody fate. Something akin, though with fewer dead, had occurred the year before at the capture of the English fort at Chouaguen on Lake Ontario. The officers that had been sent out from Mother France were disgusted with both episodes, and with the conduct of the Canadian officers who, they said, had done nothing to halt the slaughter. All Europe condemned us.

I had but a day to visit my old haunts in the city of Paris. My sole recreation was to visit the Street of the Little Gardens, where I had worked for an evening with Mr Law and first seen Jeanne de Joyeuse, at age thirteen, returned with her father from a dancing-party at the palace of the Tuileries. Mr Law's bank was now the King's Library. I was shown the place by a learned ecclesiastic with a stutter. Mr Law's cabinet and the shareholders' gallery had been dismantled and replaced by press after press of works of theology. I had not the leisure to visit the Castle of the Bastille.

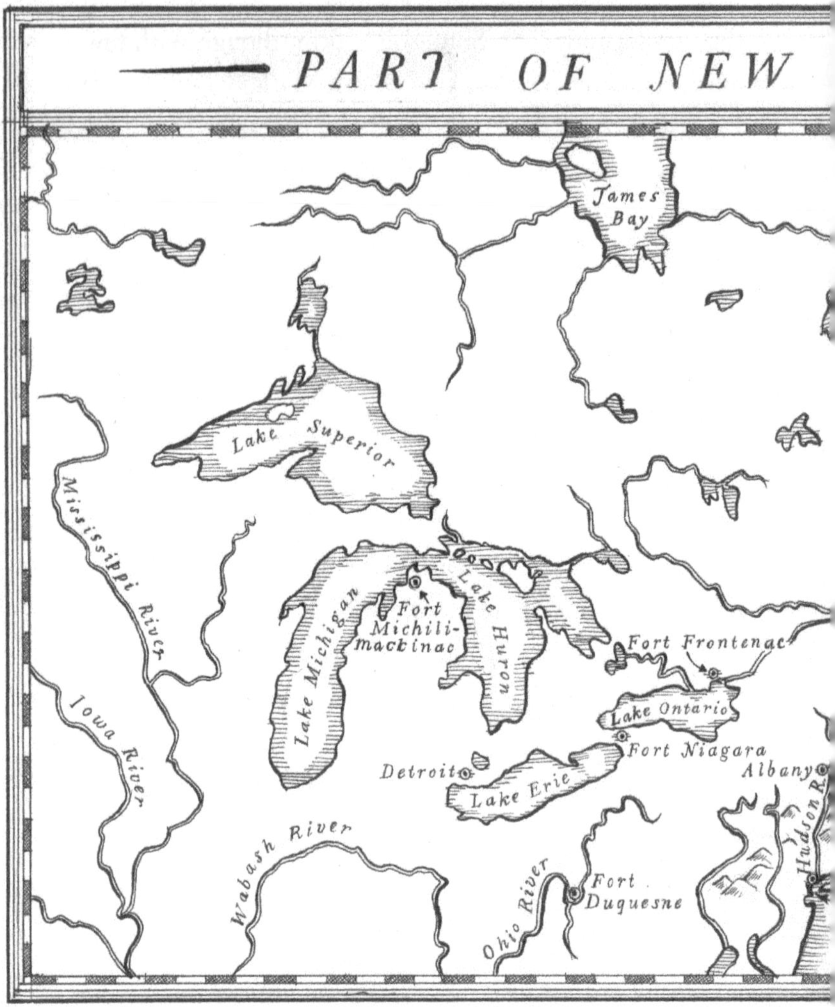

PART OF NEW

James Bay
Lake Superior
Mississippi River
Lake Michigan
Fort Michilimackinac
Lake Huron
Fort Frontenac
Lake Ontario
Fort Niagara
Iowa River
Detroit
Lake Erie
Albany
Hudson R
Wabash River
Ohio River
Fort Duquesne

FRANCE, 1758

NEW BRITAIN
LOWER CANADA
ST. LAWRENCE
Anticosti Island
NEWFOUNDLAND
Tadoussac
Quebec
Chaudière River
St. John River
ACADIA
ILE-ROYALE
Louisbourg
Montreal
Richelieu River
Lake Champlain
Fort Carillon
ake George
Boston
ATLANTIC OCEAN
ew York

PART 2

Canada, 1758

XXII

I was never no devotee of oceanic navigation. My voyage to the Indies in 1727, in the *Prince-de-Conty*, Captain Butler commanding, had ended in ship-wreck off the île de France and the loss of all hands but this sinner. The return voyage, on *L'Atalante* in 'Forty-five, had been of a piece. The finest merchant ship ever built in the yards of France, *Atalante* was at the end of her life, and so down in the water that all hands had to work the pumps in relay. Scurvy prostrated half the crew and petty officers, four of the commissioned officers, the surgeon and almoner, and the captain, the famous M. Béranger.

In that impotent state, we were all but taken by the English warship, H.M.S. *Galatea*, in a fight off the Acores. But for the firmness of a young officer named Neiret who, on his first campaign and all his seniors dead or bed-confined, had assumed temporarie command, we had gone to the bottom.

Alas! I knew just enough of open-sea navigation to have a notion of its hazardous or aleatory character. I knew a good sailor and marine-officer from an indifferent and a bad. Our vessel, the corvette *L'Aimable Pauline* out of Saint-Malo, of two hundred tons and mounting twenty-four guns, was armed for a cruise after booty in the sugar islands. Captain Chatton had been instructed by the Department to take the northern traverse, above the Acores, as less likely to cause him to tangle with the English squadrons. I froze not just from the light covering but from the evil stares of the company for which the transportation of a general officer to Canada was no recompense for rum and booty and dark women. Also, the campaign to Québec was incomparably more demanding in the navigation.

Out on the limitless sea, my regret could find no place to halt and rest. I had abandoned my happiness and left my lady without protector, my son without tutor, my daughter without ally and for what? To answer the appeal of a man and a colony of which both I knew nothing at all. I decided that such thoughts were of no use to me or anybody. I kept to my quarters, reading Father Charlevoix and other authorities on Canada, and shivered.

When consider'd from a heaving merchantmen, the contest in America appeared unequal. Not just Canada, but all of New France down the valley of the Mississippi to New-Orléans, was vulnerable. The English colonies were twenty times more populous than the French outposts on the Saint-Laurent and Mississippi. By its system of public debts, voted and guaranteed by her Parliaments, Great Britain had dug for herself an all but bottomless well of funds to sustain armies into the field and keep its forges and mills and ship-yards humming. The English colonies were expanding westwards into the interior. The Royal Navy commanded the open water.

The English had captured the peninsula we call Acadie, and with the same rigour they had shown in Scotland after the Rebellion (and, before that, in Ireland), had burned out the French *habitants* or settlers and given their farms to New Englanders. Our fortress at Louisbourg on the île Royale in the Gulf of the Saint-Laurent River could not feed itself and depended on supply from the metropolis. What had guarded Canada over one hundred and fifty years was her poverty, her remote situation and her bitter winter in which no hostile army could hope to keep itself alive and intact; and, as much as those defences, her native allies who struck terror along the English frontiers and had defeated an army of English regulars under General Braddock on the

Fair River or Ohio. That and the jealousy, one for all and all for one, of the English colonies in America.

In the course of her existence as a fortified place, the city of Québec had repelled three English attacks but that was no guarantee she could withstand a fourth. While the Court in France believed that here was just another dismal colonial fight, where any loss might be adjusted at the peace, an island here for a fishery there, a fortress for a fortress, Minorca for Guadeloupe, it seemed to me the English of America were determined to expel both us and the original nations from the continent. In the New-York and Boston newspapers such as I had been able to study at the Department of Marine, the phrase of old Cato kept surfacing: *Est delenda Carthago.*

Carthage must be destroyed.

Carthage was Québec.

XXIII

At the Banks, we lost our wind. Idle, the company fell to fishing and in no time the decks and mid-ships were knee-deep in writhening cod-fishes. Clouds flooded the whole sky. There was no sun to take the altitude at noon. The calm continued for ten days on end. I doubted that either

Captain Chatton or the helmsman had the smallest notion of our position, except that we were in the Gulf of Saint-Laurent somewhere between the île Royale and the île de Terre-Neuve or Newfoundland. Great blocks of ice, brought down from the north by the mildness of summer, hissed and clattered about us.

There was not wind enough to govern the vessel. We were drifting with the ice on the currents. The Captain ordered an anchor put out, but no sooner was it dropped that the cable parted. The crew threw out a second, but that, too, was lost. A single anchor remained.

On the fifteenth day of June, at noon, a fog came down so thick that after a time one did not know one's right hand from one's left or head from foot. The fog permeated the between-decks. Lights flickered on frightened faces and then died. Officers ceased to give orders. Captain Chatton was nowhere to be found. The sailors took to their hammocks, and I had to beat them out with the flat of my sword. One night in the small hours, the officer of the *quart* or watch called me from my cot.

Out in the gloom, my eyes could see nothing, my imagination every combination of shipwreck.

"Shall we put out the anchor?"

I thought, or imagined, a shimmer of white where the swell was breaking on reefs or a rising shore.

"No, sir."

"What is that place, General?"

There are times when an officer must display a certainty that in no wise corresponds to his ignorance, confusion and despair.

"It is the south coast of the long island called Anticosty. If you do nothing, the current will take us onto the fringing reefs."

The line of white was clearer now, like the streak of a pen across the dark. I could make out the anguished faces of the men.

"The wind will soon be with us. Kindly ring the bell. The whole company to work the sails."

I thought to feel a breath of wind on my wet cheek.

"Now, gentlemen, with your permission I shall retire. I am of the age where repose is welcome."

As I slid into blessed sleep, I heard the sails snap and rumple in the wind.

On the morrow, it grew brighter and then the sun burst through in splendour. We were afloat on a broad river or estuary, wider than any I had seen in Europe and India. Woods of pine and fir covered the banks. By one of those miracles that seemed to be my fortune in life, we had found the mouth of the Saint-Laurent. By another, Captain

Chatton appeared at noon on the dunette to take the altitude of the sun. It was 49 and one-half degrees north, which is the latitude of Rouen but by no means gave that impression. The company emerged as if from a rejuvenating sleep. A little later, we saw land on the port side which all the men swore by their favourite saints to be the Gaspé peninsula.

From now on, we would have land on each beam. That cheered the company, though we were still one hundred leagues from Québec. The navigation was slow by reason of the need for constant traverses. We dropped anchor on the north shore at a place called Tadoussac, at the mouth of the Saguenay River, where there were one or two French houses and the scaffolds and cabins of a fair for the furs brought down by the native men from the north. The road was excellent, with shelter for a fleet of ships to ride at anchor. Here, we took on a river pilot, whose opinion of both officers and crew was not at all favourable. I had nothing but admiration for M. Cartier and the other old mariners who had found their way up-river two centuries before.

At the bay of Saint-Paul, the habitations began. I saw houses of wood planks or stone washed white and before them meadows or cornfields running to the river's edge. Each allotment was the same two arpents broad. Every now and then was the gable of a little church. As we rode upstream on a light north-easter, the slope of the hills became steeper. We dropped anchor amid islands under a steep promontory called cap Tourmente. Ahead, the river was divided by a long island called île d'Orléans. Our pilot took us to the south. We rounded the island, and there, at the very limit of sight on the north bank, was a stone city that might have fallen from another world. Towers, spires, churches, convents, barracks, bastions, redoubts, hospitals, gardens and dwelling-houses rose in steep terraces from a placid bay. At the foot of the town was a clod of factories, merchant houses and river shipping. Downstream, and concealed from view up to that point by the île d'Orléans, was a high and broad cascade or waterfall.

It was the sight that had come to me, in a premonitory dream, in my cell of the Inquisitors' prison at Venice in 'Forty-seven. I said to myself: "So here, dear friend, at the end of the earth, we shall remain. Let us make something of this finale."

XXIV

After taking leave of my ship-mates, where no regret was wasted, I climbed the perpendicular street to what is called the High Town in search of M. le marquis de Montcalm.

I found him absent on campaign at the head of Lake Champlain, some eighty leagues to the south and west. There were orders for me neither at the Admiralty nor at the Intendance. M. Vaudreuil, the Governor General, was at Mont-Réal, his ordinary place of residence, fifty leagues up-stream. That officer was not expected to come down-river to the capital until the spring where it was his practice to await the first vessels from the metropolis so as to answer the correspondence from the Court. Nobody in Québec had expected me nor knew who I was, but I could see that none cared for the look of me. On July 2nd, 1758, I took passage up-river on a brigantine bound for Mont-Réal. Our good north-easter scuttled us along.

M. Montcalm's victories at William-Henry and Chouagen had, it appeared, made a favourable impression on the Canadian nations. At the gate of a wretched fort in a bad situation called Chambly, we came upon a camp of native men, from an up-country race called Outagamie, three hundred strong, armed and provisioned for war and preparing to set off up the Richelieu River to join M. Montcalm at the fort of Carillon at the southern end of Champlain. I attached myself to that force, not exactly in command, but nor entirely in subordination.

New France is girdled in woods, and protected from attack except by water: by the Saint-Laurent, where the navigation was as difficult as it might be, by the long lakes to the south called Champlain and Saint-Sacrement and by Lake Ontario to the west. The citadel of Louisbourg on the île Royale had been erected to control the mouth of the river, while Fort Niagara commanded the passage between the lakes of Ontario and Érié, and Fort Frontenac the approach to Mont-Réal. Further to the south and west, Fort Duquesne overlooked the Ohio.

The royal troops, amounting to a ration-strength of some three thousand, comprised the battalions of La Reine, Béarn, Languedoc and Guyenne, which had been sent from the metropolis at the outset of the war, and those of La Sarre and Royal-Roussillon that had come with M. Montcalm in 'Fifty-six. At Louisbourg were a further eleven hundred men of the battalions of Bourgogne and Artois. Two thousand marines and, at maximum, two thousand Canadian militia completed our strength. (New-Orléans was so distant that she could no more reinforce Canada than we could come to her succour.)

The English could place in the field twenty thousand regular men, and half as much again of militia. The winter in their colonies being less severe, they could set their forces in motion in spring some two or three weeks earlier than we might, but must carry their ordnance and supply across some of the most unforgiving country on earth.

The Canadians appeared to me to be good soldiers, able to subsist on very little, and admirable shots. As for our native allies, if my experience in India might still be of any value, they must regard the war as not principally their affair and of importance only in so far as it were beneficial or noxious to them. The English could offer better goods in gifts and trade, but we had the advantage of the Roman Catholic faith which seemed to appeal more to American notions of the supernatural than the Calvinism of Boston. Eight generations of Jesuit and Récollet fathers had chosen to live among the native men, learn their speech, tend their invalids and share their joys and miseries. In contrast, as far as I could judge, the English hated and feared the ancient peoples of America.

Yet, as always in such affairs, the natives would ally with the stronger party.

XXV

Canada is no place for wounded men. The passage up the Richelieu was slow, by reason of a strong wind from the south-west, and by rapids where all hands had to take up and carry over broken ground the canoes and gear. On the second day, a great mob of voyageur pigeons flew over and the men made great slaughter by simply discharging their pieces at the sky. It was not what the English call sport, but the fowls made a fine dish stewed in a mess of myrtles and blewberries.

All around was sunlight and vacancy. It seemed to me that in this wilderness, you might not fight as in Europe, in ordered corps and brigades and divisions. Number was less valuable than quality. A small force, lightly armed, well-led and -provisioned, familiar with the woods and waters, could hold at bay a mass of unseasoned European soldiers with their cumbersome formations and road-bound supply-trains. Forts, of which both belligerents appeared greatly fond, were quite as useful as gangrene, for the defenders must starve, or mutiny, as they had at Louisbourg in the late war, or desert to the enemy.

I thought that one must fight like the native men, who had brought a style of warfare over centuries to perfection. One must fight in skirmish lines, taking advantage of the contour of the ground, and of the cover of brush, crag and timber. Attack would be much harder than defence, for defenders were ready, in cover, and knew the lie of the land at their front; while the assailants must needs grape their ways over every sort of local or prepared obstacle under directed fire. If attack were difficult, retreat I thought near impossible. What had to be avoided at all cost was the sort of pitched battle of Europe. Victory brought small advantage and defeat no decisive consequence.

As I puffed and lumbered, I thought: The most important quality of a commander of soldiers is not luck, foresight, courage, dash or care of supply. It is passable health.

XXVI

At the spit called Pointe-au-Fer, we entered the great lake of Champlain and launched the canoes. Three were unsound, but there remained thirty-eight, each capable of carrying nine men and their arms and supplies for three days. The going was easy across the placid surface of the lake but, as the heat of the day came on, I sensed an alteration in my companions. Their faces, never of the most expressive, became set. Their chatter died away. The paddles in the water made scarce a sound. Flocks of teal came scuttering over the water towards us, but no man raised his weapon.

I smelled the war before I heard or saw it. Somewhere in advance of our flotilla, the woods were burning. From our right, smoke was creeping over the water. Then I heard the grumble of cannon, and then musket-fire, single shots and rolling volleys, the roar of burning brush, and the screams of wounded men. The Outagamies laid their oars

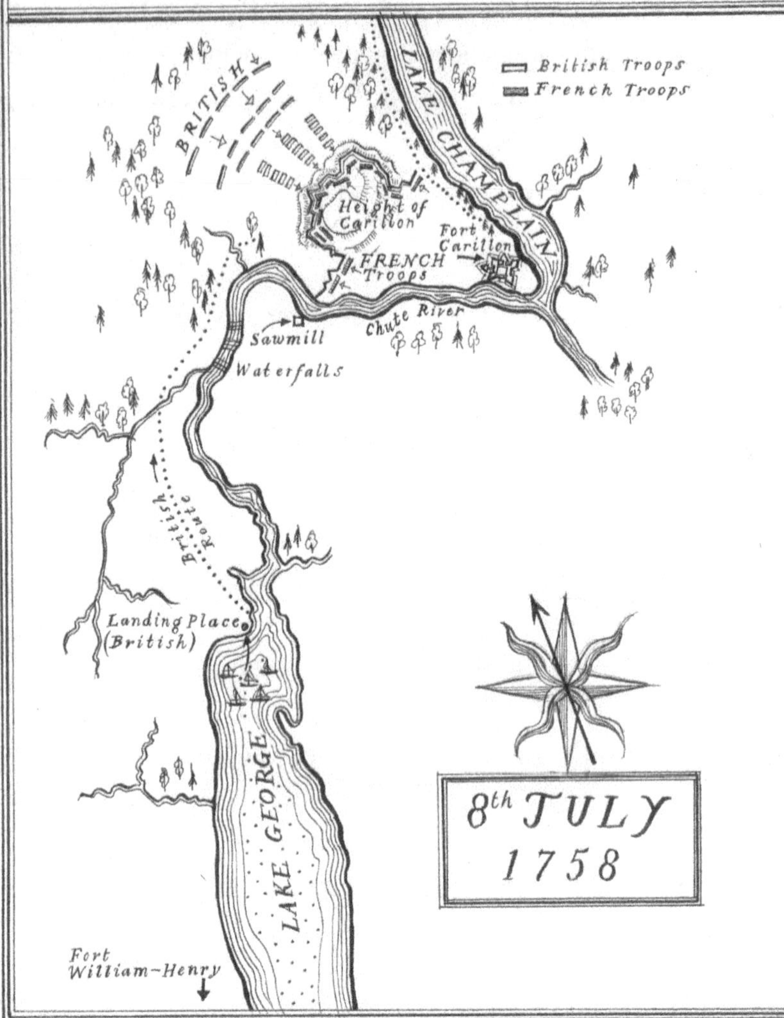
BATTLE OF CARILLON
British Troops
French Troops
BRITISH
LAKE CHAMPLAIN
Height of Carillon
Fort Carillon
FRENCH Troops
Chute River
Sawmill
Waterfalls
British Route
Landing Place (British)
LAKE GEORGE
Fort William-Henry
8th JULY 1758

across their knees. In the great solitude, the only sound and movement was a battle to the death.

I gestured for the canoes to close up, and spoke distinctly.

"I beg you, gentlemen, not to encumber yourselves with prisoners and scalps. There shall be plenty of both and to spare should we prevail. We must cut through the English in one stroke for we have not the numbers to stand and fight. Select a point just to the lake-side of the enemy centre, so that we may cut off a weaker section which may lose heart or fall to a sally from the fort. Feel at ease to make us much noise as you are able.

"Now, kindly light your matches. By reason of old wounds, I am slow. Do not wait for me but be at 'em as soon as we beach."

I do not know if they understood me. The smoke was so dense I could scarce see the man before me. Then, with a horrid sound, the canoes grounded and the men were springing out in a tumble and running into the trees.

I caught up at the edge of the wood. Before us, through the low branches and rolling billows of smoke, was a battle of a ferocity such as I had never witnessed. To our left, on a slight elevation, was a breastwork of felled trees, of nine or more feet in height, so that I could see no defenders but only caps, musket barrels and the standards of our battalions. At its foot, all along its length was a tangle of brush, and close against the works, a criss-cross of sharpened stakes, which our siege engineers call an *abatis.* Impaled on it, like prey in some wood-shrike's larder, were the bodies of English grenadiers and Highlanders in every posture of death and agony. The whole ground was on fire and men were scuttling out with buckets and axes to keep the flames from the walls of the breast-work and the abatis. The sun was a dull disc. To our right, across the cleared ground, musket-fire flickered from the trees like summer lightning. The battle must have been in train for many hours.

One of the men was surveying the field, quarter by quarter. I nodded to him and said:

"At your order, sir."

The warrior pondered a moment, and then halloo-ed set to wake the dead. Our force burst from the wood like a pack of greyhounds off the leash. Through the smoke, I could see Highlanders running in every direction. Their officer tried to turn them and was felled by a hatchet. From the top of the breastwork, Frenchmen as black from smoke and blood as veteran devils were roaring in joy and encouragement.

To our right, across the cleared ground, at the margin of the unfelled wood a gun-shot away, an English officer with a drawn sword was haranguing a mob of native men.

An Outagamie lad raised his musket and took his aim. Before I could stop him, the haft of his captain's hatchet came down on the barrel and the ball went into the brush.

The English officer continued his exhortation, with his life but without success. Then he was overrun by men in retreat. At the wood's edge, some turned, to loose off a parting shot, and then vanished.

The Campbell men were throwing down their arms and running at me.

"*Thugam, a Ghàidheala! Thigibh mum chuairt!*"

Come to me, Scottish lads! Gather about me!

From behind the rampart of the breastwork, I heard a *porte-voix* or loud-hailer.

"William, is that you?"

"M. le marquis?"

"Do you speak French, dear friend?"

"A few words, sir."

"Take your men to the head of the Portage and forestall M. Abercrombie bringing down his heavy guns."

"Yes, sir."

I turned to the native captain. "What under Heaven is the Portage?"

"Viens."

Come.

Having entrusted my prisoners to a lieutenant of La

Sarre, we set off. We came to a burn, where barges lay splintered or up-ended by our cannon shot. To our right was a magnificent water-fall that, at any time but the present, I might have stopped to admire. At the base of the fall was a saw-mill in flames, and a half-mile of fast-running water where we crossed on rocks exposed above the race.

"Gentlemen, I want pickets to a bow-shot each side the main body. There will be groups of English stragglers, some of them numerous."

"Guil! Non!"

William! No!

The warriors looked at me with what seemed close to puzzlement. I sensed that they did not, at that moment, require instruction in woodland warfare. Should they ever once do so, I would be among the very first authorities they would consult.

"Very good. Carry on, gentlemen."

I turned to my new friend. He was in the prime of life, tall, at least six feet, and well-shaped, with long hair that perhaps he had never cut and atop it, with an excellent effect, a European bag-wig. His face was splashed or piqued with vermilion and his bare chest rubbed with the grease of some animal or plant that smelled most savoury. About his neck was a silver medal with a portrait of His Christian Majesty, a lady's hand-mirror and an iron crucifix. A Tulle musket, clean and polished, completed the warrior's armament.

"May I enquire your name, sir?"

"Powattamie."

"I am fortunate to have you at my side, sir."

"T'es boiteux, Guil."

You are lame, William.

"Alas! So I am, M. Powattamie, but my heart is strong."

"Porter?"

Carry?

I felt that to be transported on the warrior's shoulders would not enforce my slender authority with the native men.

"I shall march at my own pace, M. Powattamie."

I thought: This Portage will be the death of me. One would need a body of iron to survive in this country.

XXVII

As we proceeded, I could hear, from in front and across the stream, the confused sounds of a force in great disorder.

I said: "I need guards at every landing-place on this shore."

The men looked up and, with scowls and shruggs, some

of their number slipped through the trees. I suspected that they found my prudence bordered on poltroonery; but they would, in a spirit of military experiment, comply.

“Les Anglois sont vaincus, Guil.”

The English are beaten, William.

Ahead, in the gloaming, I could see a make-shift bridge over the river, scattered at both heads with discarded gear and the litters of wounded men. I thought: If we place ourselves between the English army and their landing-place on Saint-Sacrement, we could cause General Abercrombie no little inconvenience.

I could see no force to guard the bridge, but to the right was a thicket of bushes, not unlike our European bay or laurel. The men fell to a crouch. Then something took off my hat in a swoop, and the thicket burst with flame.

I now had the leisure to observe the native men at their work. Their tactics were ingenious. A man would show himself, and as he drew fire, a dozen others would roll round their tree-trunks and get off a shot into the muzzle-flashes.

“Vingt-sept fusils.”

Twenty-seven muskets.

I was no less surprised than M. Powattamie. The force was by much too small to protect the embarcation. It occurred to me that some conscientious officer, and a very few good men, had been ashamed by the disorderly retreat. Their fire was diminishing. With what remained of their powder and ball, the English men were seeking to kill me and M. Powattamie. I could hear the voice of their officer.

I surmised we had an half-hour of light. I had read somewhere that the native men of Canada do not care to fight in darkness.

I was about to propose an enveloping movement, when I saw between the trees that it was complete. I heard again the English officer.

I shouted in English: "Mr Harris! My people are behind you. If you lower your weapons, I shall preserve your brave soldiers."

"What! And let your hairdressers at them! No, by heaven!"

I said in Persian: "I am coming towards you, Mr Edmund. Will you invite your men not to shoot me?"

I walked towards the English. The anger of the native men rolled in gusts and broke on my back as if from a fire of thorn. I sensed, from the sweet smell, that M. Powattamie was behind me, walking arsewards, covering my skull and back against a hatchet. Mr Harris stepped out from behind a white pine tree. His hands and face were a mass of cuts and scratches. He reversed his sword, which I did not take. One by one, his men crept out from their caches.

I shouted: “The English chief spared my life in a battle across the water. I now spare his life that we may be enemies once more.”

There was a clatter of voices on all sides, which then subsided. It seemed my action, to an extent, accorded with what they felt was right.

“M. Powattamie, please inform the gentlemen that they shall receive from me in ransom for these English soldiers precisely what the King of France pays for their scalps. They shall also have my friendship.”

I do not know what M. Powattamie said, but I caught the word Ononthio, which is what the naturals call His Christian Majesty’s Governor General.

There was a whoop and the men were racing to the bridge.

“Les blessés.”

The wounded.

“Bloody hell and damnation, Edmund! How could Abercrombie leave his wounded!”

“He left them, General Neilson, because he believed that the French officers had a shred of honour and would protect them.” General Harris raised the hilt of his sword at me. “Men! This is Neilson, the blackest traitor that ever lived, cruel, ungrateful, a Jacobite—”

"I am not a Jacobite, Edmund."

"If your lady could see you now fighting like a savage . . ."

"Right. That does it. Lord Powattamie, would you be so kind as to kill and scalp the English general?"

Relieved that the ordinary system had been restored, that captain unsheathed his knife and raised his hatchet.

"All right, I take that back. Admit you are a Papist."

M. Powattamie halted in mid-slaughter.

"I am, Mr Harris, and so is Lord Powattamie. I advise you to be careful what you say about our cult."

Mr Harris was swaying with weariness.

It was now too dark to proceed.

I said: "English men! We will descend by the river to the French camp. If you cannot carry your wounded, you must despatch them. Mr Harris, you are to stay at my side."

To be agreeable, I said: "You said you were ordered to India."

"I was, but the Secretary at War thought my knowledge of the Persian language would be of greater service in the North American theatre."

"In that, Mr Barrington was correct."

Already morose, Mr Harris fell into silence. His mood can barely have been improved by M. Powattamie, who was proddling him in the back with his hatchet, and repeating:

"Arrie! T'es captif de guerre. Oo-oo-oo."

General Harris! Prisoner of war!

To relieve poor Mr Harris, I turned to my native friend.

"M. Powattamie, would you enlighten me on something? How do you talk to the men of other nations? I have heard you, an Outagamie, speak with Mohawks and Senecas and they understand you."

"Jargon."

"Will you instruct me this winter in the jargon, sir? I would have you by me all the time, and live with me the whole season. I shall honour you and reward you as you deserve."

We crossed again at the smoking saw-mill, and climbed up to our retrenchments.

In the desolation of burned ground, M. le marquis de Montcalm was seated on a stump. He appeared to be asleep. About him, staff officers lolled or dozed in their shirts.

I spoke up: "M. le marquis, may I present the gallant General Harris, who sacrificed himself and his brave men to cover Mr Abercrombie's retreat?"

M. Montcalm awoke. He stood and said: "Who has not heard of the exploits of the famous Edmonde Harris? But you are wounded, sir."

"Only in my self-esteem."

"Oh, come now, sir. Such are the fortunes of war. A glass of eau-de-vie for the brave English general!"

"I have promised my lady not to touch strong liquors."

M. Montcalm thought for a moment. He said: "Perhaps, sir, if I give you my parole, and order my staff officers to do the same, then Mme Harris shall never hear of your unprecedented lapse. But why, o why, did Mylord Abercrombie not bring down his heavy cannon?"

"That is a military question that I am not required to answer."

"Of course. Pardon my curiosity, General Harris."

I sensed a certain impatience, in both M. Montcalm and his officers, that Mr Harris was not more grateful to have retained possession of his fine head of hair.

"I must see to my men."

"Of course."

Once he had set off, attended by two native lads, I turned to M. le marquis de Montcalm.

Louis-Joseph, marquis de Montcalm, was a handsome, well-made man, eight or ten years my junior. In the two late wars, he had fought with bravery on the Rhine, in Italy and Austria, and been wounded five times. After thirty years of service, he had retired on a pension to his lands at Candiac in the Languedoc. I was told at the Palace of Versailles that M. Montcalm at first declined command in Canada, not least because he would be under the orders of M. Vaudreuil. After a time, he was persuaded that his appointments as maréchal de camp, and a rich pension, would give security to his lady and numerous family.

I said: "May I congratulate you, sir, on your great victory? The English are in no state to advance their cannon. You have bought with blood and exertion another year for the colony."

"I am overjoyed, William, that you, and you, M. Sans-Gêne, arrived in time to witness this unusual engagement."

I had thought that M. Powattamie and the native men had done rather more than simply witness M. Montcalm's triumph. Having as yet no skill in Canadian physiognomy, I could not judge how my new friend received M. Montcalm's declaration. His face betrayed neither thought nor feeling. In fairness to M. le marquis, he had fought for five hours amid prodigies of fair conduct by both officers and men, while we had brushed in for the final act and the applause of the house. We were the pin dropped on an even balance that had sent it tumbling down.

The nikname Sans-Gêne means "unabashed". I understood that M. Montcalm, in thus addressing M. Powattamie, intended to license the chief's very free way of speaking but restrict it to him. For who among the native men was so valorous in battle and so wise in council? I was William to show I was an intimate relation, else how had I been placed above Canadian officers of merit? He presented his officers, of whom he especially marked M. le chevalier Lévis and M. Bougainville.

"If we survive the year, William, the campaign will have been fine and glorious."

Not so.

"Sir, will you give orders to muster two hundred men, Canadians and naturals, with supplies for a month, powder, lead and snow-racquets, the whole to be ready to march with me before dawn?"

M. Lévis said: "Mr Abercrombie will have sent to fortify Albany. Already, the native men are leaving camp with their booty."

"I shall not go to Albany. I shall descend the Hudson River on its left bank to New-York. We will lay waste the farms in the Broncks and New-Haarlem, take command of the Broad Way and burn the shipping in the harbour. The English will not be in a condition to mount an attack on Québec next summer."

"Les vivres, Guil. L'hiver est nostre ennemy. Pire que Corlar."

Supplies, William. Winter is our enemy, worse than the English.

"We shall not winter in the territory, gentlemen. We shall leave New-York in our rear and march into the warm lands and winter at New-Orléans. When the snow-water has passed, we shall paddle up the Mississippi River. You may send our orders to Stinkards' Bay or the Détroit."

M. Powattamie made a sound that might have been laughter. He said: "Guil est vieux, Marquie. Il n'est pas sot."

General Neilson is old, sir, but he is no fool.

"Can you muster the men, M. Sans-Gêne?"

"J'en doute."

I have my doubts.

The chief rose and left us.

M. Montcalm looked at me with diffidence. "How is my cousin, M. Neilson?"

"Not best pleased with you, sir."

"What could I do, William? You have seen how matters stand here. Also," and here M. Montcalm lowered his voice so none but I could hear him, "you should know that the Canadians are quite impossible to manage, let alone the savages. You are the most experienced officer in our service in the direction of native auxiliaries—"

"You flatter me, M. le marquis."

". . . and are not Canadian. This war must be fought on European tactical footing: plans of campaign, divisions, artillery and sieges, pitched battles directed by experimented general officers sent by the Court. Enough of these ignoramuses and empirics!"

Since I belonged to both those latter categories, having had no military schooling and learned my craft in command of a band of English deserters on first setting foot in India in 'Twenty-seven, I thought it prudent to keep my peace. I now saw why M. Montcalm had brought me across the Atlantic: to direct the native men, and bear the ignominy of any cruelties on their part, while he might fight as if he were in Flanders or on the Rhine.

M. Montcalm smiled at his show of bad humour. He said: "Meanwhile, you have captured for me an English general officer."

"I shall let him go."

"On his parole?"

"No, sir."

"Arrie a fait grâce à Guil. Au-delà de l'Eau."

Mr Harris spared Mr Neilson's life on the other side of the ocean.

That was one of the native men.

M. Montcalm shook his head. I sensed that the democratic, even Athenian, character of staff work in North America was not at all to his taste. "Whatever you gentlemen do, do not inform me of it."

I saw that I had made a satisfactory impression on our

native allies, but could not for the life of me descry how I had merited that honour. I had not distinguished myself in the battle. Indeed, I had not drawn sword. At the head of the Falls, I had prevented what promised to be an agreeable massacre. I resolved that whatever I was doing to the taste of the native men, I should continue doing it.

XXVIII

Mr Harris stepped in, in a knot of native lads and torches. He appeared to be at the end of his wits.

M. Montcalm said: "General Harris, you are free to return to Guillaume-Henri but your men shall remain."

To forestall Mr Harris, I said: "I shall make their welfare and protection my especial care. If Mr Abercromby agrees to an exchange of prisoners, I shall ensure that it is executed in perfect security."

M. Montcalm said: "General Harris, you may take an escort of two private soldiers."

"They will not leave, sir. They think they shall be scalped."

I turned to M. Powattamie. "Would you kindly detach a guide to lead Mr Harris and me to the English fort?"

"Pouf! Je te montreroi la routte moy-mesme."

Nonsense. I shall myself guide you.

Harris sighed. He said: "William! Abercrombie has vowed to hang you from the first convenient tree."

"Nanby va fair pendre Guil! Powattamie va écorcer Nanby!"

Mr Abercrombie intends to have William hanged? I shall myself flay Mr Abercrombie!

M. Montcalm scowled. I suspected that he regarded our native allies as a necessary evil but without love or esteem.

I said: "Well, that gentleman will have to capture me."

M. Montcalm had fallen into thought. After a time, he said, more to himself than to his officers:

"Until this day, in more than one dozen campaigns, I fought for my honour and glory. Today, with no possibility of retreat or succour nor, after the affair last year at Guillaume-Henri, any hope or right of quarter, I fought for my life."

The night was warm, and pine branches made an excellent couch. I woke at dawn to M. Powattamie's firm grip on my right arm.

"Ils sont partis."

They have left.

XXIX

At the landing, all was confusion. The whole western shore of Saint-Sacrement was encumbered with the smoking wrecks of barges and pontoons, dismounted cannon, boots and muskets stuck fast in the mire, abandoned shelters, wounded men thrawing on the bare ground. Two of the Outagamie had brought up a light canoe, and lifted me into it as if I had been a child.

M. Powattamie knelt in the stern, and steered us into the early mist. Facing each other, Mr Harris and I fell into conversation.

I said: "You should leave us at least the valley of the Saint-Laurent and the lower Mississippi. Else it may go ill for Great Britain in America."

I droned on: "It has happened before that a colony overtops its metropolis. You remember Carthage and Tyre; and Byzantium and Corinth. For the moment, your American colonies are happy for you to exhaust your Exchequer to destroy our French positions, while they jaw away in their assemblies. Five years from now, or ten years at most, they shall throw off all subordination. Your countrymen in America are poor friends, but they shall be bad enemies."

Mr Harris did not appear to be listening. I gave up.

"Shall you tell Mr Pitt what I have said?"

"No. Fuck off."

"I thought as much."

M. Powattamie had taken no part in the political debate though, out of politeness, it had been conducted in French. He appeared to be lost in his thoughts. He looked up and spoke.

"Pour quoi les François sont ils venus dans nostre Terre?"

Why did the French come into our land?

"I am the worst person to ask, M. Powattamie. In truth, I do not know."

"Nous sommes point allés vous chercher, ni vous, ni Corlar. Vous nous avez demandé de la terre, parce que celle de vostre Pays estoit trop petite pour tous les hommes qui y estoient. Nous vous avons dit qu'il y en assez avoit icy pour vous et pour nous, qu'il estoit bon que le mesme Soleil nous éclairât, que nous marcherions le mesme Chemin. Quel besoin avions-nous des François?"

We never went out to fetch either you or the English. You requested land of us, because your country was too small to hold all the people who were there. We said there was land and to spare for you and us, and that it was good that the same sun should shine on us both and that we together tread the same road. What need could we have had of the French?

Mr Harris said: "The French bring you muskets and powder and cloth and wine and vermilion and looking-glasses and brandy."

"Pah! Avant eux ne vivions nous pas mieux que nous ne faisons? Nous servions de nos arcs et de nos hâches, qui suffisoient pour nous faire bien vivre. Pour couvertes nous nous passions avec les peaux de Bêtes fauves qui sont plus chaudes que leurs couvertes blanches, bleues ou rouges. Nos femmes travailloient à faire des Couvertes de plumes et d'écorce de bouleau. Pour boire nous buvions de l'eau pure, jamais l'Eau forte qui nous rend fous. Avant l'arrivée des François, nous vivions comme les hommes qui sçavent se passer à ce qu'ils ont, au lieu qu'aujourdhuy nous marchons en Esclaves qui ne font pas ce qu'ils veulent."

Bah! Before they came, we lived better than now. We had our bows and hatchets which more than sufficed to give us a good life. For blankets we made do with the skins of wild beasts which are warmer than their cloths, be they white, blue or red. Our women worked to make cloaks of feathers and birch-bark. For drink we had the pure water, not this poison that robs us of our wits. Before the French came, we lived as men who know how to be content with what they possess while nowadays we are like slaves who may not do as they please.

Mr Harris said: "The French brought you the crucified God."

"Ach! Si Powattamie eust esté au pied de la Croix, il jure, ils n'eussent jamais réussi à tuer son Seigneur."

Ach! If Powattamie had been at the Cross' foot, by God, they would never have succeeded in killing his Lord.

"We know that, Mr Powattamie, and, incomparably more important, He knows that."

Lord Powattamie scowled. Yet it seemed that Mr Harris, by his diplomacy, had restored some of the warrior chief's humour. He said:

"Parlons d'aut'chose, mes frères."

Let us speak on other themes, my brothers.

The wind had dropped. The hills, splashed with green and yellow and, here and there, the bright red of sweet maple, came back at us from the water as from a looking-glass. Only the dip of M. Powattamie's oar disturbed the surface. I thought: In such a world, Hector and Achilles fought, and Helen loved and Andromache grieved.

I said: "Is this not, M. Powattamie, the loveliest place on earth?"

"C'est pas. Autre part."

Not at all. That is another place.

Mr Harris woke from his thoughts. "Will you show us

one day that other place, Mr P.? After we have buried for all time our axes in the ground."

The chief looked at Mr Harris and, then, at me.

"Accordé," he said.

Granted.

Powattamie sprang for his musket and, with a groan, toppled into the water. I threw off my cloak and weapon and dived after him. As I plummeted under the weight of my legs and boots, I saw musket balls shooting through the water and then dropping about me. My hands plunged into the warrior's streaming hair. I kicked against his back and, horizontal, slowed our descent. We began to rise and burst through the surface.

I saw Mr Harris upright in the canoe, seeking with his person to shield us from the musket-fire from the western shore. On the water's surface was a ribbon of blood from M. Powattamie's wound for all to see.

"Breathe in!"

We descended. I could see the spent shot rolling off the face of M. Powattamie's coat.

We rose again. We were in the lee of an island, which gave us cover from the shore. The firing diminished and then stopped. I trusted that Mr Harris had reminded his countrymen of the Riot Act.

I lifted M. Powattamie onto a spit of shingle. The

place seemed to have been much used as a port of call by the naturals, for pulled out and beached were the remains of two canoes amid the skins of beasts and the ash of old wood fires. In examining my patient, I found that the ball had missed the artery but broken on the thigh-bone. I cleaned the wound as best I might, and cut my coat into ribbans to restrict the bleeding. During the surgery, M. Powattamie did not move. Then, he pushed me away, made as if to stand, fell back on his hanches and began to howl.

"I beg you to keep silent, M. Powattamie, as far as you are able."

The warrior looked surprised. "Chanson de mort, Guil."

"Damnation your death song, sir. You are not going to die. In place of that racket, which will bring the whole of the English army on us, you will instruct me as to how to repair this foolish canoe."

M. Powattamie looked long into the trees and then, after consideration, pointed at an immense white birch which had no low branches. I paced the better of the two broken canoes and, under my companion's instruction, cut a sheet of bark some twelve feet long and four feet in the breadth. I had to make a scaffald to make the higher cuts. While I was at work, M. Powattamie dragged himself on his elbows to the broken canoe, pronounced its timbers sound and cut off the old bark. I carried my roll down to the shingle, gathered stones to hold it open and flat, and placed the ribs of the old canoe atop it. To cut the joinerie short, I shall but say: M. Powattamie sent me for pine-roots and spruce sap, with which he sewed and caulked the vessel. The enveloping woods were chittering with grouse, and a kind of squirrel, tame as a lady's lap-dog. With a hail of pebbles, I took enough to make my patient a passable bouillon. I cut some fir boughs for his bed.

After dinner, I said: "Shall we wait for first light, M. Powattamie?"

"Non pas. Je seroi mort."

No. I shall be dead.

"Nonsense. But let us set off now."

Brilliant starlight doubled off the still water. M. Powattamie showed me the celestial body that marks the north in these districts, and I kept the bow of the canoe always beneath her. He lay in the bottom, breathing with a horrible rasping. The birch let in not a coffee-cup of water.

The dark banks began to close in on us. The boat bumped against an obstacle, and then others, which were dead Englishmen. I landed the canoe as neatly as a native.

"Now, M. Powattamie, if you will be so kind, I shall

place you on my back and we shall toddle down the Portage path to our friends. It is a dander of but two leagues."

"T'es boiteux, Guil. Laisse-moy."

You are lame, William. Leave me.

"Nonsense. I shall carry you and we shall do very well."

M. Powattamie was a big man, with a weight of perhaps fifteen stones. After no more than four or five hundred yards, my ankles defeated me.

"We shall make a small change in system. I shall walk twenty steps and then rest, then twenty more, then rest, and we shall be at the camp in no time."

I counted eighteen, then slipped and fell with a crack on the stones. Powattamie let out not a cry. I rose, and lifted the warrior onto my back.

"Now, M. Powattamie. Shall we not count our steps? One . . ."

"Deux . . ."

"Three . . ."

"Quat . . ."

I fell again. We lay, together, gasping on the stones. I rose onto my knees and tried to raise him but I had no more strength.

"Guil? Chanson de mort?"

William? Death song?

"I think that would be very much in order,

M. Powattamie. With your permission, I believe I shall join you. My own death song is a pleasant air from my country, of some little age, entitled: 'Neighbours Farewel to His Friends.'"

"Nae come is my departing time . . ."

"Estenniayon-de-tsonwe-iesow . . ."

"And heir I may nae longer stay . . ."

"Onnawatwa-d'oki . . ."

"What I have done for WANT OF WIT . . ."

"N'ONWANDASHWAENTA . . ."

"TO MEMORY, I'LL NOT RECALL . . ."

I suspect that emulation is human nature. While I disliked M. Powattamie's wail, so he detested my trill and we wasted in outsinging each other those dregs of strength better reserved for the saving of our lives.

Yet, I believe it was our rattle, varied by an occasional punch and kick, that caused two private soldiers of La Reine battalion, out without leave on the hunt for booty, to find us at each other's throats and raise the alarm.

XXX

Once I had the use of my legs, I found the camp as busy as a bee-hive in sunshine. In our absence on Saint-Sacrement, the fires had been stamped out, the dead buried and the breast-work repaired and raised yet higher. I reported to M. Montcalm that, from my observations on our jaunt, it was my belief the English would not enterprise a second assault. I said that, in my judgment of the debriss, the English had lost more than a thousand men, and a great many junior officers. (Those last, unlike general officers, are not easy to replace.) I had seen no native casualties and suggested that the Iroquois men had been content to tarry at the rear of the English columns and await the outcome of battle.

For all that I had advanced closest to the English retrenchments, my advice was not accepted. The English prisoners said that they had been told that the withdrawal was but temporarie, and General Abercrombie intended to return with cannon and a better disposition. The passion for fortification won the day. Also, our French regulars, officers and men, had fought the battle of the lives and it would stay in them, like a shiver of steel or stone, for a good long time.

The staff officers that had come from France with M. Montcalm were courteous. Whatever they thought of me as an officer of fortune (as we say), Scottish, of a dubious nobility, and fighting as a savage among savages, I had arrived to halt a battle that otherwise might still be being fought. If M. Bougainville, who frequented scientific companies at Paris and London, was surprised the learned Mme Neilson had allied herself for life with a Scotch gowk, he kept that sentiment to himself.

My concern was M. Powattamie and the safety of Mr Harris' men and the Highlanders, to whom I had given my word. The morrow of my return, M. Vaudreuil's brother, M. Rigaud, landed with a force of some six hundred Canadians, Iroquois and Abénaquies. The native re-inforcements, who had been held back by M. Vaudreuil for a raid down the Mohawk valley that had been deferred, were in the very worst of humours. They had missed a great battle and a heap of booty and scalps, which had fallen to, of all the most despised nations, the Outagamie. The late-comers were determined to have their share. They stalked about the English prisoners, like butchers in the cattle pens at Falkirk fair. The Outagamies, though adopting something of a superior air with the newcomers, were true to their chief and provided a sort of guard for the English and Scottish captives.

With M. Montcalm's permission, I set off with the chief surgeon, M. Beauchesne, to enquire after my Outagamie friend. The native loges were strung along the lake shore. At the entrance to the native camp, M. Beauchesne vomitted.

"Look ahead of you, M. Beauchesne. Do not look to the side."

We were shown to a cabin at the extremity of the camp. The indoors was full of smoke from a fire of pine that a lady was fanning with a paddle. Lord Powattamie was stretched out on a pile of animal skins, breathing with the greatest difficulty. He made as if to sit up, but fell back. The evening light cut a bar through the smoke.

"Guile. T'es mon frère."

William, you are my brother.

"Indeed I am. I have brought M. Montcalm's surgeon, M. Beauchesne."

"Non. J'vais aut'part."

No. I am going to the other place.

"No, M. Powattamie, not yet! I shall carry you over to France. You shall live in ease and honour in my lady's woods and I will come each evening at sunset to smoke a pipe with you."

"À Dieu, Guil."

The lady rose from her hanches and began to scold.

"À Dieu, dear friend. Come, M. Beauchesne. We are not required."

Outside in the dusk, a party of young men formed a sort of horse-shoe figure about the lodge. The lads eyed the surgeon's satchel. One came forward.

"Donner eau! Eau!"

Give us water! Water!

There was a roar of approval.

"Eau! Eau! Eau!"

Water! Water! Water!

I crossed my arms and said: "Life-water is for warriors. Not for idlers who skulk in their loges. Did I see you in the fight at the abatis, sir? Or in the action at the head of the Falls? I did not. Step out of my path, you prattler."

It was conjecture, which turned out to be accurate. The men slunk away, leaving but three who were beholden to the orator, or especially thirsty. They shook down their hatchets.

"M. Beauchesne, when I fire, you are to recharge each pistol as soon as you receive it."

There was a stammer. "I do not know how."

"Never mind. Just look as if you know."

There was a moment of utter silence; and then, from the cabin, the sound of song which I believe to be the noblest music I ever heard. It was the death song of a man who leaves life as a man rises from table, or passes from one room to another. Powattamie was leaving his wound on earth. He was going, hale and strong, to his Lord. The eyes of the lads flickered like a dying fire, and then went cold as ash. They turned and, without a backward look, stalked away.

After a while, M. Beauchesne said: "I am a physician, not a fighting man."

"You did very well, M. Beauchesne. Years from now, you shall tell your grandchildren that one time in America, you went with old Neilson to treat a famous native warrior dying of the gangrene and, though that man refused treatment, you learned more that day of physick than in all your study and experiment."

I have seen before that once an episode can be dramatised, or made into a story whose composing parts are true in themselves, it is more easy to bear. M. Beauchesne became cheerful. I imagined that, in a sort of dialogue with himself, or in the manner of an expert painter, he was adding to the tale some little spots of colour and movement. I caught him stealing glances at me so that he might note my dress and gait. He looked up to take the weather. By the time we reached M. Montcalm's general-quarter, we were the best of friends.

XXXI

The summer days elapsed in clavers, incompetent or deceitful interpreters, bare knives and haggles. To let some steam out of the kettle, I sent out raiding parties which returned, after a day, empty-handed or with a single scalp divided into four. I had hoped to do some botanising for Mme Neilson, but no plant or simple gathered off the mountain was the price of a split skull.

In near despair, I proposed, as a more vigorous diversion, a match between Iroquois and Abénaquie of the camping game called Crosse or La Crosse.

The game is played with a round stone and clubs shaped in such a fashion that they seemed, to the devoted Reverend Fathers of the last century, to resemble the instrument of Our Lord's passion. The stone is placed between the two parties or nations, and each seeks to drive the stone to the antagonists' goal while defending his own goal. In modern times, the match is played without edge-weapons, a reform that some of the older men judged a degeneracy. A space was cleared on the esplanade below the redoubt and M. Montcalm ungraciously endowed a prize of necklaces and beads to a value of one thousand crowns.

M. Abercrombie was on his high horse. In a message, brought from William-Henry under cartel by a lieutenant of grenadiers, the English commander said that without instruction from the Court he was willing to exchange only officers. Though M. Abercrombie's force outnumbered ours by four to one, he seemed reluctant to allow us any augment. As luck would have it, I came on a native man with a miniature portrait of a beautiful lady, the wife of an English officer who had fallen beneath the abatis. For a heap of tobacco, I acquired the picture and passed it *sub rosa* to the English lieutenant. (I thought it better not to write to Mr Harris, lest I bring on my friend a suspicion of treasonous intimacy with the enemy.)

As often with small and meaningless gestures, the poor widow unlocked the door. A second parlementaire, attended by thirty Highlandmen, agreed to take Mr Harris' men. It was no great matter to attach to them the Campbells, whom Mr Abercrombie could scarcely with honour send back up the lake to us. By a happy coincidence, the prisoners set off up the Portage path amid the roar and tumult of the Crosse match.

M. Montcalm's aide-de-camp, M. Bougainville, who had been much at London and spoke English better than I do, conducted the exchange from our side. He was permitted to disembark at William-Henry and was not blind-folded until he was inside the retrenchments. On his return with our paroled prisoners, he seconded me in my optimism. None the less, M. Montcalm seemed determined to remain at Carillon and turn the place into an American Namur. I have never known a camp so given to false alarms, day and night, generally night. I suspect that the English fort was no more serene. Thus both commanders, convinced against all evidence of their adversary's superior strength, prepared for an attack that would never come.

On the sixth day of September, couriers arrived from both Québec and Mont-Réal. The first brought news of the surrender of the fort of Louisbourg, and the second of the fall of Frontenac. The consequence of our caution was obvious to all. Some of the officers put on a brave face. The fortress at Louisbourg had held long enough to prevent the English fleet proceeding to Québec. At the peace, should it come this winter (they said), Louisbourg would be handed back to us in return for Port Mahon in Minorca, taken from the English in the first year of the war. I believe only M. Montcalm shared my certainty that this was a battle to extinction.

I learned something of my native friends. In past years, the Outagamie nation had been notorious all over the high country for treachery, deceit, theft, incest and anthropophagy; and had been in unremitting war with the French since the earliest days of the colony. In about the year 1750, a young Jesuit priest, Father David, had walked into their winter camp and, though hung by his feet for three days over a slow fire of thorns, had shown no distress but rather rejoiced to be sharing in his Master's martyrdom.

My friend, then a lad of some seventeen or eighteen years, was so touched by the young priest's bravery that he sprang into the fire, cut the religious down, and stood astride the all but lifeless body, vowing to fight any man who sought to prolong his torments. Father David did not long survive his ordeal, but in that time conveyed to his rescuer the rudiments of the Catholic faith and a devotion to the person of Our Saviour. Elected chief, M. Powattamie had brought his nation into alliance with the French. He had been in the fight at Fort Duquesne that killed poor Braddock in 'Fifty-five, and saved M. Montcalm's life in the slaughter at William-Henry in 'Fifty-seven.

The Outagamie were restive. As far as I could understand, they wished to return to the Détroit to bring in their corn. I proposed to travel with them downriver to Mont-Réal, and present myself and them to Governor General Vaudreuil for inspection. We would then gather what we could by way of powder, ball and victuals, pass over the Rapids into Ontario and along the south shore of the lake into the upper country or pays d'En-Haut, carrying the report of M. Montcalm's victory as we went. The exsequies for M. Powattamie completed, the election achieved and the harvest stored, we would place ourselves in ambush in the woods at an equal distance between Forts Duquesne and Niagara, ready at an instant to harry any English move against either place. I had concerted the project beforehand with M. le chevalier de Lévis and M. Bougainville and the plan came back at me from M. le marquis as his own. Such is the merit of efficient staff work.

There remained a ceremony in which M. Montcalm, after incessant prottling from me, "covered" the body of the gallant Outagamie chief with presents. For all that we set off in the canoes amid dirges and threnodies, the men showed every sign of pleasure to be quit of the mixed company of the fort.

XXXII

Mont-Réal, the commercial heart of the colony, lies beneath a butte or cliff on the north-west shore of the Saint-Laurent, a little downstream of the first rapids. Established in the last century for the trade in pelts with the pays d'En-Haut, the place is but a village, where all conditions live hoggledy-piggledy behind a defective rampart. I was reminded of the Edinburgh of my early years.

Two long, unpaved streets run in parallel with the river, joined by narrow vennels. Most of the houses are affairs of wood. There are five churches and, as always on French ground, as many convents. The unbuilt spaces are given over to gardens and pig-sties. A little industrial suburbs or Fauxbourg to the west comprises a flour mill, a boat-yard, a cider-press and a brew-house. I saw no carriage or any horse. The foot-passengers were mostly soldiers on their private affairs, voyageurs returned with furs from the Détroit and Michilimackinacke and sisters of the different religious orders. News of Mr Montcalm's victory had preceded me, and every person I encountered was eager to tell me about it.

M. le marquis de Vaudreuil, the Governor General of the colony, had been Governor of Louisiana at New-Orléans, and had done much to improve that colony after the failure of Mr Law's projects of colonisation. Though but a captain of vessel in the French marine, he outranked M. Montcalm.

At Carillon, the officers who had come out from Mother France spoke of M. Vaudreuil with amusement. His fault, as far as I could determine, or rather the capital fault from which all others descended, was that he was Canadian. M. Vaudreuil had married some time before a lady who was not only without fortune, but also fifteen years his senior: a combination that my brother officers found rustic to the point of clownishness. Both M. and Mme Vaudreuil were known to be devout, never a recommendation in His Christian Majesty's service.

The inspection was to be at the place d'Armes, which did a second duty as a market-place. The ceremony was delayed for a reason it took me time to disentangle. As far as I could gather from the native men, the election of their chief was hemmed by ancient and precise regulations. In the vacancy, it were of the first importance that there be no presumption of the result of the election. The master-of-ceremonies requested that I myself should represent the nation before Ononthio. I declined, twice, lest my performance as orator give M. Vaudreuil a false impression of my standing with the Outagamie and with the nations in general. Voices were raised, whether in anger or distress I could not determine.

In the end, I saw there was no way past the constitutional problem. I submitted and did my best. M. Vaudreuil treated the Outagamie with much tenderness and distributed presents like a Homeric hero. He then received me in private audience in one of the very few houses of stone with an inside staircase. We snugged in a sort of cabinet while Mme Vaudreuil wrote letters at a corner-table.

I had been told that M. Vaudreuil and M. Montcalm differed in their strategical philosophy, but the division went far beyond military affairs to every aspect of existence. Had one ever said it was day, the other would have called for lights and tapers.

The battle at the abatis had been won, it seemed, not by the French regulars but by the native men and the militia. Why had M. le marquis de Montcalm not fulfilled orders to move on William-Henry? Why had the men that he, M. Vaudreuil, had sent to Carillon been employed cutting trees, digging holes in the earth and consuming rations that the colony could ill spare? Of his contempt for the staff officers from the capital, the Governor General made no secret. He excluded only M. Lévis and, for no better reason than some septentrional affinity of Canada and Scotland, me. Having no skill in intrigues and cabals, I murmured inaudibly.

My orders for the western expedition M. Vaudreuil over-ruled, on the ground of the advancing season or simply because they had been presented under M. Montcalm's sign-manual. I was to await the arrival of the battalions of Berry and La Reine from Carillon, and carry them up to winter at Québec. I was to oversee, in conjunction with M. Bigot, the King's Intendant, the fortifications of that city against an assault next year that was all the more to be expected as the consequence of M. Montcalm's inaction.

On my taking leave, Mme Vaudreuil took my hand and said: "Ménagez vous, monsieur, je vous prie: nous en avons besoin."

Take care of yourself, sir. We need you.

The Outagamie offered two young men as hostages for their return to the low country next spring. I feared I might not be able to feed the lads over the winter and again declined. We parted on excellent terms. The transports of the regulars were not easy to assemble and the first snow was falling when, on October 6th, 1758, we set off downriver for Québec.

XXXIII

As we descended in flotilla, I saw ice was beginning to spread out from the banks. Idle, I repeated in my head the same set of questions.

How was it that a colony such as Canada, established more than one hundred and fifty years before, blessed with a good soil, where every man could have as much land as he was able to clear of timber and put under cultivation; was free to hunt and fish where he pleased; paid no taxes to the King; how was it that such a colony could not feed its own forty or fifty thousand inhabitants, far less export a surplus to the mother country or the isles? Meanwhile, the English colonies thrived, and were pushing the western frontier down the valley of the Ohio.

The Greek cities were narrow places with a hard, dry

soil and scant pasture, and if prosperity brought an overplus of people, there was no ground to sustain them. The colonies those cities founded, at Syracuse and Naples and Byzantium, owed no subordination to the mother city, made their own laws and alliances, set their own taxes, fought their own wars. In contrast, France had no surplus of population and, in Mr Law's time, had resorted to raking the prisons and bawdy-houses of Paris and the greater provincial towns to populate Louisiana. France, England, Spain, Holland and Portugal had fallen into the detestable import of African slaves.

Kingdom or commonwealth, the states of our times had established for their colonies monopolies of trade which enriched a few merchants but beggared the colonists and raised the price of provisions in the metropolis. The most prosperous commerce was in disease. It had been better that none of the latter-day colonies had been set on foot, or that they had at once been sent out without recourse, like morose cadet sons.

I had with me M. Vaudreuil's despatches to the Court at Versailles, in triplicate, and the letters of Mme Vaudreuil and the other Mont-Réal ladies to their parents in the metropolis. Those would be taken across the Atlantic by M. Bougainville on the last ship to leave the road in the first week of November. I prayed that there would be a letter awaiting me at Québec saying that Mlle de Joyeuse and M. Duclos were married.

XXXIV

At Québec, I called first at the évêché or bishop's palace. Mme Neilson had proposed, for the greater security, that she write by way of M. l'abbé de L'Isle-Dieu, the episcopal agent at Paris, who had most kindly agreed to convey her letters in His Reverence of Québec's packet, and transmit any replies I might have leisure to write. I had no doubt that Mme Neilson intended that I might sometimes attend Mass at the Cathedral of Québec, both to convey to Bishop Pontbriand my obligation to him, and to please my devout correspondent.

No letter awaited me, and the ecclesiastical visit gained for me only a false reputation for both tact and piety.

I had better fortune at the Intendance, in the suburbs of Saint-Roch where a tributary river called the Saint-Charles debouches into the Saint-Laurent. M. Bigot, the King's Intendant, entrusted with justice, the management of commerce and the finances, had the air of a commis who had impoverished himself in His Majesty's service and now faced entire ruin. An efficient administrator, he had about him a spectral train of damned souls to do his bidding, of whom he recommended to me M. Péan and M. Cadet, who were, if anything, even closer to famine. All had inherited departments in indescribable chaos. All were in bad health. All had begged the King for permission to return to the metropolis to repair their constitutions and fortunes. Models of probity in small matters, they were as ripe a pack of rascals as one could hope to meet.

From my life as a young man in another of our colonies, the île de France, I took their grumbles with a grain of salt. In contrast to that starveling isle, Canada offered ample opportunity for self-enrichment. A colony that had cost the Court but two millions in 1730 was now consuming ten millions for the expenses of the King's establishment here and in the île Royale, the pay and provisions of the regiments and gifts to the nations. Very little of the King's bounty was reaching its destined recipients. I had seen at Carillon the wretchedness of the supply, the poor nourishment, bad tobacco, stinking deer-skins and shoe-leather, thread-bare capes, breeks and leggings, and rusted axes, spades and mattocks. As for the gifts to the nations, perhaps two-thirds remained in Mont-Réal while the remnant was trucked for their private purposes by the commanders of the posts in the High Country.

M. Bigot and his friends, united in a co-partnery called

the Society or Grand Society, enjoyed exclusive concessions to buy furs at the trading posts at Stinkards' Bay and Lake Superior, a monopoly of both inland shipping and the sale of timber to the Antilles and the opportunity of contraband trade with New England. With M. Vaudreuil and M. Montcalm on bad terms the one with the other, there was no superior authority to bring those officials to heel.

What was to be expected of a colony where the principal officers, endowed with an arbitrary authority and entrusted with the King's funds, monopolised trade to the exclusion of the colonists? Was such a colony, more ruined than ever Sicily by Proconsul Verres, worth preserving?

I had often seen in life that the most self-interested of men consider themselves the most put-upon. M. Bigot and his myrmidons disliked Canada and the Canadians and had no intention of settling on this side the water. They saw themselves as Atlases who had preserved a neglected colony from foundering; and since to do so they had put at risk their estates, their daughters' dowries and their posterity, they merited a commensurate reward. Indeed, they might at times have argued that the fault lay not with them but with a monarchy that had never, in its glorious history, possessed money or credit to match its martial ambitions.

The King of France has no gold or silver mines. He may

sell annuities to his subjects, and pitiful honours, charges, offices, judgeships, bishoprics, governances, colonelcies and inspectorates. He may encumber his Court and public administration with do-nothings. He may levy duties on every species of cloth and edible and convert France into a nation of smugglers. He may tolerate every sort of tyrannical conduct in his servants just so long as a share of the evil fruits come into his Treasury. He may declare himself bankrupt every fifty years, like the Hebrew Jubilee. Yet, he will still need money.

The King's authority was an illusion. His palaces, fortresses, armies and colonies were emblems not of sovereignty but of servitude. The King was the slave of his subjects. It would be wiser, I thought, that His Christian Majesty recognise his subordination and tax his subjects not by fraud and violence, but by their consent. The King of France must grant his subjects a parliament and delegate to it sovereign authority over his outgoings.

I did not think it proper to give vent to those democratic nostrums.

While I was hirpling about the woods, M. Bigot must have had some intelligence from Mother France, for he questioned me about the canal on Mme Neilson's lands. I discoursed on the engineership until heads sunk on chests and the ladies stamped their feet. Poor folk do not generally dig canals of fifteen leagues in extent. I could see that those little saints were mortally afeared that Mme Neilson might enter the Canada trade and bring capitals to bear that would jostle their partners at Bordeaux, La Rochelle and the other metropolitan ports. They might have heard whispers from Versailles about Mme Neilson's banking project.

I set their minds at rest. I said that the canal would not return its lost fund for many years, if ever, and that Mme Neilson had embarked on the scheme less in the hope of gain than out of public spirit. That last phrase seemed unfamiliar to my auditory.

I wondered if those gentlemen might do me a bad turn. The spirit of caution, which had become my besetting fault, caused me to cast about for reinforcement.

I rode out on the Sabbath to a village called Jeune Lorette, some one and a half leagues north and west of the town. A remnant of the Huron nation, driven by the cruelties of the Iroquois from its home country up-river, had been domiciled there in the last century on a fief of the Jesuit fathers. They had built for themselves wooden houses *à la françoise* (as we say) and a rude stone church.

Their numbers, no longer restricted by the surface or extension of their hunting lands, or the depradations of the Iroquois, had over time augmented to some two hundred families or one thousand souls. Over the long years, they had mingled with the habitants and English prisoners of war, and taken (it was said) many children that certain families of the town wished out of general sight. The young men spoke French and the women displayed a mastery of the most vivid insults in that expressive tongue. Devout and biddable, the Hurons of Jeune Lorette yet possessed a martial spirit.

With the agreement of Richard, their chief or orator, and of the Reverend Fathers, I embodied some ninety or one hundred of the youths into a sort of marshalcy to keep order and attend fires in the lower town. Their operations, attended by their hunting dogs, assuredly did not add to the love for me in the commercial quarters. I also proposed, as any experimented soldier might, that the stores and warehouses be brought into the rear or land-side, and the whole lower town, excluding the church of Notre-Dame-des-Victoires, be razed to provide a glacis on the river-side. I could not win M. Bigot to my proposal but rather made myself yet further detested. One good consequence of this proposal was that, in an unusual harmony of spirit, M. Montcalm and M. Vaudreuil wrote from Mont-Réal to give me a more precise idea of my duties, suggesting that I leave off engineering and concentrate my forces on our native allies.

The victory at Carillon had added further to M. Montcalm's prestige. I do not think that France had ever stood higher among the native men. The matter was not to stage a Triumph but use that elevated standing in the service of the colony and Mother France. I had in mind a congress of the nations, to be held as soon in the spring season as possible at Jeune Lorette. The Iroquois nations on the borders must be persuaded to enforce their neutrality so that the English might not pass through the lands. I believed I could have won M. Powattamie to a project of sanctuary and fair conduct for women, children and the wounded. Without him, I was not sanguine.

I missed M. Powattamie. In my landlouping life, I had met some outstanding men: Mr Law, Captain Bigby, Father O'Crean, the musician Ezéchiel, Joseph Durfort, King James Stuart. M. Powattamie overtopped them all. The world each one of us inhabits is not identical, but fashioned by the formation of our minds. Each impression we have of touch or scent or sound is strained through a myriad anterior impressions, unique to each one of us. M. Powattamie's world seemed to me the purest and, for all his life of violence, the most generous. M. Montaigne wrote in one of his essays that we should judge no man until we have seen the manner of his dying. I had seen

Powattamie die and must seek, in a manner how inferior so ever, to follow his pattern.

XXXV

I rented a house, rue Sainte-Famille in the upper town, for the happy sum of 1,500 livres per annum. It was a stone house on two levels, not unlike the houses of the better sort I remembered from Brittany, but smaller. Sparsely furnished, with a stove in iron and brick, a pair of oak chests for linen and gear and coarse Bergamo tapestries on the walls, it was cosie enough for me. One room served for my bedroom and cabinet and another as *salle de compagnie* or receiving-room. The kitchen and offices were separated across a small yard of apple trees. M. Bigot graciously offered me the use of some of his plate, of which he must have had a surplus. I was determined to have no obligation to him, and declined.

My hostess was a widow-lady in the most profound dejection.

"Will you not sit a moment, Mme Bouchard? You seem sad. If I can do anything to alleviate your sorrow, will you say?"

The lady looked at a chair, and just as soon looked away, as if it had ceased to be her property.

"No, sir. Why should I need anything?"

"Come now, madame. I am a stranger here. I have no friends in Canada, except . . ."

I had an inspiration.

". . . except you, madame."

"I am a poor widow and . . ."

And?

Mme Bouchard sat down on the corner of the chair.

We were advancing.

Mme Bouchard dissolved in tears.

". . . and I have lost my daughter."

I said nothing.

"Done to death . . ."

I said nothing.

". . . by a damned assassin, damned to Hell for all time."

I brought up the other chair and sat down before her. I said: "Kindly tell me what occurred."

Mme Bouchard became alarmed. She said: "I have deposed a process-verbal at the Intendance."

"Speak to me, as you would to your dearest friend."

The story came out all in a tangle but, by supplementary questioning, I was able to arrange it in a sort of order. Adeline Bouchard, sixteen years of age, not tall nor yet small, fair-haired, pretty as a picture, was a good student at the college of the Ursuline sisters, rue Saint-Louis. On

September 17th, while I was at Carillon, it being a Sunday, Mlle Bouchard was not in her place at evening prayers. A search was made of the chapel and the convent buildings, and the porter sent out to scour the surrounding streets. By next morning, the whole town was roused. Not a trace was found, and as the days passed, spiteful people wondered if Adeline had not eloped with a young man into the woods.

Then, the next Saturday, a countryman vaguing on the beach below the Falls of Montmorency, saw what he thought were abandoned clothes. Climbing down, he found the lifeless body of a young girl. He believed she had fallen from the head of the Falls, or been washed ashore from upstream. Beside the poor girl, tied with a gay ribbon, was a spray of flowers.

"What flowers were they, madame?"

Mme Bouchard looked at me in a sulk. She had given me so much and seemed to feel in the exchange very much the creditor.

"What colour were the flowers, madame?"

I seemed to be standing at the very gates of Hell.

"Wild-flowers. Yellow wild-flowers. They do not have a name."

"Madame, I give you my word before God that I shall find your daughter's assassin and give him and you the justice you both deserve."

Mme Bouchard stood up. I do not think that she believed me. I offered to escort her to her lodging, but she seemed eager to dispense with my company.

I sat down and gathered my wits. I had thought, in my self-centred vanity, that the attack on Mlle Marie-Ange at La Ferté in 'Forty-seven was concerted so as to give me the frights. So it was, but there were other impulses at work, dragged up from the depths of our evil nature, which in the wilderness of America had brought forth their hideous fruit. M. le comte de Luynes had killed poor Adeline for pleasure.

I said to myself: "This shall be your last duty before getting off the stage: to give justice to the murderer and some little consolation to Mother Bouchard. You shall find M. Luynes and fight him. Saving Canada is beyond your powers. You shall, with the remains of your strength, achieve the smaller charge."

XXXVI

My first port of call was the Intendance. M. Bigot kept me waiting for ten minutes, an interval I judged to be calculated to show both his diligence in the King's affairs and his courtesy. Long engaged in the Atlantic trade, his family had passed, by way of the parlement of Bordeaux, into the nobility. It was said that he had remitted much of his gain in Canada back to that city, had bought a seigneurie in the country nearby and would bury his own and his family's commercial past in lands, woods, vines and armorials.

M. Bigot said: "Such things unfortunately occur, and in places better policed than America. A fellow tries to steal a kiss, or more. The lass don't like it. There is a tussle, and the wench is hurt."

He turned away and, as a sort of favour, gave me a confidence. "Indeed, M. Vaudreuil informed me that such a thing occurred at New-Orléans while he was Governor there. A young girl, of a good family of Havana, I do not recollect her name, Doña Ana something, was found by the ship-yard on the river, strangled, and with every evident trace of having been violated."

He turned back to me and said: "General Neilson, there are very few men who are perfect. The service is replete with men who are of great value to the King and yet very bad at heart."

"M. Bigot, if we cannot protect the daughters of honest bourgeois, we might as well sail away and see if the English can do better."

"That is sedition, M. Neilson."

"No doubt, sir, but it is also the plain truth."

"I do not believe that M. de Vaudreuil or M. de Montcalm would wish you to pursue this matter at the expense of your command."

"I believe, sir, that I am the best judge of how I employ my energies."

I had no better fortune at the Ursuline sisters. Mère de Saint-Pierre graciously consented to receive me. The convent stands in a lane off the rue Saint-Louis. I was shown by the porter into a little room, white-washed, swept and bare of furnishing or decoration but for a chair and, in the opposite wall, a window covered by a wooden grille and, beyond that, a curtain. After a time, the curtain was drawn to the side. As far as I could judge through the bars, and the swathes of black cloth about the face, Mère de Saint-Pierre was a lady of very advanced years, in uncertain health.

I learned that Mlle Bouchard was a model boarder, neat, courteous, exact in her observances, and an excellent embroiderer. She left the convent only on high days to attend Mass at the Cathedral. The only visits she received were from her mother.

Mme de Saint-Pierre said: "What is your interest in this evil matter, General Neilson?"

I replied, truthfully: "I have lived a soldier's life, madame, for thirty years and done much that will weigh against me in the judgment of Heaven. I wished to have one good act to place in the balance."

"We shall pray that your wish be granted, General Neilson."

I had hoped for forensic assistance, but one must take what is offered.

XXXVII

On the morrow, November 8th, word came that a merchant vessel had been seen off cap Tourmente. My house was a tangle of contradictory intelligence which unravelled into *Junon*, of three hundred tons gross weight, out of Lorient in Brittany, Captain Veiret commanding, with supply for General Neilson. From my vantage, I could see men climbing onto roofs to wave their hats and, from below, boats putting out from the lower town. A little later, a sailor waddled in and said, in Breton, that I was ordered aboard. It was some time since I had been given a direct order, and I snapped to it like a recruit.

Out on the water, I had been preceded by the cutter of M. Bigot's Society. I could hear and then see above the deck-rail a marine officer berating the munitionnaire,

M. Cadet. I saw, with delight, that M. Veiret was none other than my friend Neiret from the last voyage of *Atalante.* I climbed up into the row.

"I am on the King's business! General Neilson, kindly explain that to this obstinate officer!"

At the hint of sport, sailors began to collect about us.

"Alas! M. Cadet, I have no authority on this vessel."

Captain Neiret spoke: "You are trespassing on my command, sir. If you do not return to your launch, my men shall throw you into it, or the river, whichever being more convenient."

Two volunteers stepped forward for that duty.

With a look of something like panic, the official scuttled off and down.

I glanced at Captain Neiret. The slender youth had become a marine tyrant. Wind and sun had taken the bloom from M. Neiret's cheeks, but had made him strong as a pollard oak. Beneath his right eye, I could just make out the mark of the spent ball that hit him in the fight with Mr Baker off the Acores in 1746. Otherwise, in contradistinction to other fighting sailors, he appeared to have the ordinair equipage of eyes, teeth, ears, noses, arms and legs. I resisted the urge to embrace my young friend.

"Do you have letters for me, M. Neiret?"

M. Neiret gathered himself. He walked to the rail. I followed him. He looked at the dock and just as soon turned away.

He bent his head towards the water and said: "On my departure, Mme Neilson gave me a verbal message for you. It is: 'M. La Porte, the first commis at the Department of the Marine, intercepts all Canadian correspondence for the Secretary that concerns the activities of the Grand Society. Would General Neilson kindly convey his particular wishes to Mme Neilson and she shall ensure they are transmitted to the Court?'"

"No affectionate superscription, M. Neiret?"

That officer looked startled. "No, sir."

"Nor intimate, but proper, farewell?"

"No."

"Would you be so good as to carry to Mme Neilson a cipher for this correspondence?"

"Of course."

We made our way to the council room. As we stooped to enter, I said: "How was the crossing, M. Neiret?"

"Plain sailing, as well it should be with such a complement of officers as these gentlemen."

M. Neiret presented them. They seemed no older than the Chevalier.

"Unfortunately, Mr Drummond and the *Dromadaire*

struck on the reefs and returned to Lorient for reparations. I thought it better that we make our own way alone."

"Thank you, M. Neiret."

One of the lads piped up. "Do you speak English, M. Neilson?"

"I do, M. Ponponne. I learned it at my dear mother's knee."

"Then, sir, may I ask: what is the English for *rejeté*?"

There was merriment among the lads.

"I see you have been spinning yarn, M. Neiret."

"I have told the gentlemen how, back in 'Forty-six, by a stratagem, you captured the English first-rate, H.M.S. *Galatea*, mounting seventy-two guns, Captain Jeremiah Baker commanding."

"It was not my doing, gentlemen, but that of your captain at fully fifteen years of age."

The officers gazed at M. Neiret in adoration.

"Is Mr Baker yet with us?"

One of the boys stepped forward. "The gazettes have Admiral Baker living in retirement at The Bath, where he is much in requisition of noblemen and ladies."

"So that is all right then."

Amid the clatter, I saw that my friend was agitated. I thought at first that he was vexed at being taken, red-hand, in telling battle stories. He was shooting glances through the panes.

"Shall we take the air, M. Neiret?"

"Will you excuse us, gentlemen?"

From the dunette, I searched the dock for the cause of M. Neiret's discomfort. It was not hard to descry.

"You mind the tall girl with brown hair, standing a little apart from her friends."

M. Neiret blushed. "I had not remarked her."

"Do you not think you should raise your hat to the young lady, M. Neiret? Without affectation."

He did so. There was a tumulte among the girls, except the brown one, who took a step back.

"And replace it."

He did so.

"Do you think she saw, Mr Neilson?"

"Yes."

"How shall I find her, Mr Neilson?"

"You need have no anxiety about that."

XXXVIII

I passed the morning at Jeune Lorette, overseeing the stowage of the cargo in the church and the hangar abutting it. There was sure to be shrinkage over time, but nothing like the reduction that would have occurred in

M. Cadet's magazine. Thanks to Mme Neilson and Captain Neiret, I had supply and merchandise to the value of some 80,000 francs and 30,000 francs in presents for the native people.

At my lodging, there was a letter awaiting me from Mme la comtesse de Brillard de Saint-Anne de Châteauguay, inviting me to dinner that day and proposing, if it pleased me, that I bring the young captain of vessel lately arrived.

In Canada, the mass or volume of a personal name stands in inverse proportion to the respectability of its owner. M. Châteauguay possessed a seigneurie of six leagues square above the Rapids, but inclined to spend his summers in the woods, running with his native compers after beaver, trucking eau-de-vie and attending to his forest wives. I had seen him once in the firelight below the walls of Québec, his bare trunk piqued with ash and vermilion. Mme de Châteauguay was poor even by the standards of the town, which is very poor, so I sent my maître d'hôtel and cook with provisions, candles, linen, plate, firewood and Champagne.

I had long been aware that sailing men are helpless on the terra firma. As we climbed to our rendez-vous, M. Neiret traned like a lazy scholar, fidgelled with his latchets, tie and wig, and stopped at every corner to point out *Junon* aswim on the broad bosom of the Saint-Laurent.

The guests were few but among them was Father Laval, Jesuit, expert on the natural history and native tongues of Canada, whom I had long wished to meet.

Mlle de Châteauguay was dressed as she had been on the dock. She was finer in close than from afar, strong, graceful, smiling and fairn-tickled from the sun. She looked at M. Neiret and, without taking her eyes from his face, dropped a curtesie.

They were placed side-a-side at table. There was no fanfaronnade from the one, nor from the other coquetterie. Each questioned the other. After a while, no doubt satisfied by the answers, they fell into a silence. Every now and then, each would study the other's face, rather as an officer on march consults a map.

"Come, Mme la comtesse. A hand of lansquenet, if you please. Let us leave the young persons to their chatter. Will you not join the card party, Reverend Father?"

"I shall observe the hazards by M. Bernouilli's system, but not play."

My hostess was an expert and ruthless player, and I quickly lost full fourteen sols. Looking above the lady's head, I saw, on the overmantel, a vase of yellow flowers.

"What are those charming wildflowers, countess?"

Mme Châteaugay glared at me and traced with her finger on the cloth the French word for "rival".

Father Laval looked up from his notes. "I have classified the plant *Lysimachia ciliata.* It is our Canadian primrose."

Jean Duclos, where are you when I need you?

I gathered the cards, stood up and stepped towards the visionaries.

"Mlle de Châteauguay, will you permit an old soldier to plead the cause of his friend Jérôme Neiret?"

"You are named Jérôme!"

"Yes," M. Neiret stuttered. "I can change it, I mean, if you do not care for it."

"Not at all, sir. I like it. I like it very much. I am Agnès."

"Agnès!"

I had lost them.

"Please listen to General Neilson, dearest."

"Yes, Mother."

"M. Neiret is the most capable young officer in the French Marine. With God's help, and yours, he shall rise to the highest dignity and you shall live in happiness and honour. But first you must cross the water. Are you brave, mademoiselle?"

"By the Chalice, my daughter is, General. I remember once a white bear—"

"Please, countess. I would like to hear Mlle Agnès say it."

"Yes, sir. I am brave."

"You shall need to be. Once at sea, you will know fear and danger, and sickness and filth and hunger and thirst and insult and ugliness such as you could never have imagined from the dry land. The incessant rolling of the vessel will make you wish you were dead. You will be soaked in salt water and shivering with cold all day and all night. M. Neiret will not be able to attend to you, for every sinew in his being will be committed to preserving his command. Yet whenever he needs you, you must be at his side. If there is a fight, which is likely, you will fight or else assist the surgeons, which is no more agreeable. Can you do that, mademoiselle?"

"Yes, sir."

"So! With your agreement, Countess, and yours, dear Reverend Father, tomorrow, in the parloir of the Ursulines, exact at noon. I have sent word into the woods to avise M. le comte. Should my people not find him, I shall myself beg the honour of attending Mlle Agnès to the altar. I shall ensure M. Neiret is washed and brushed and on time."

"I have no dress or bonnet, sir!"

"Your friends among the pupils and the novices are at this moment at their needles."

Outside in the mud, Captain Neiret turned on me in fury. I forestalled him.

"Mlle Châteauguay is in immediate and mortal danger. Only you can protect her. You must be wedded and set sail no later than tomorrow's tide. I feared that your esteem for her, and your wish to honour her father and mother might—"

"Danger? Explain yourself, man, for pity's sake."

"I cannot. Mme Neilson will explain once, with God's help, you both are in Old France. I have set six men in ambush, two at the front of the house, two behind and two in the Place."

As if to order, one of the men slid out of the dark. M. Neiret, who had surely never seen a Huron armed for war, showed admirable calmness.

"Sois tranquille, Nerrie. Nous sommes en faction."

Have no fear, M. Neiret. We are on watch.

"If Mlle Agnès is in danger, I must be with her."

I restrained him. "No. Tonight, Mlle Agnès is our charge. Tomorrow, she is in your care, and for all her life. Come, dear friend, I shall take you to my lodging. You must look well for tomorrow."

"For God's sake, tell me!"

"Some months ago, Mlle Agnès' friend Adeline Bouchard was assassinated. I was at Carillon with M. le marquis. On my return, I looked into the matter. I have ground to believe that a like fate is this moment being prepared for Mlle Agnès. I have promised Mme Bouchard that I will find and kill her daughter's assassin, and so I promise you."

He looked dazed.

"Do you have money, M. Neiret?"

That officer blushed. "I have Mme Neilson's bill on M. Le Ber."

"Shall you not expend it on your wedding-feast? And a gift to the good sisters?"

"Yes. Mr Neilson, I must go back."

"Yes. Do not attempt to give orders to the native men."

XXXIX

After the homily and the blessing, we passed at the bride's request into the burial-ground where she laid her bridal posey on Adeline's grave. Already placed there was a spray of yellow flowers. Père Laval was in tears, and I thought to see, in M. Bigot's eye, a beamy moisture. I feared I might spill my entrails and stepped back from the grave.

My house was illuminated, inside and out, and there was meat and drink to feed the whole hungry town. I was so distrait that I fear I fell short in my duties as host. I thought: How is that a man who had kept his head when

Mlle de Joyeuse was in danger has lost it now? I ascribed my weakness to the accumulating foolishness of old age. Truly, match-making is the final senility.

After some time, one of the native men brought me a letter, written in blood or berry-juice on birch-bark. I carried it to the bride, who was seated amid her friends while M. Neiret's officers stood in line-astern, launching indiscriminate gallantries. While my young friend decyphered the sylvan epistle, I took M. Ponponne aside, saying that there must be no auxiliary nuptials or any affair that might divide the glory of Mlle Agnès's day.

The bride smiled and passed the message back to me. She said:

"M. Neiret shall, it appears, be rich, though not, I think, before the nineteenth century."

"With your permission, mademoiselle, I shall read it to the company."

"Oh no, sir!"

"It must be published, mademoiselle."

With a shiver of pain, Mlle Agnès nodded.

"Ladies and gentlemen! Attention, if you please! Mlle Agnès has commanded me to read the following communication: 'By these presents, I the undersigned Hubert de Châteauguay, counsellor of the King in his councils et cetera, being detained on business on my Canadian estates, hereby constitute as my general and special attorney Mr Major-General Neilson, Scottish gentleman and knight commander et cetera, resident at present at Québec; to whom I give the power for and in my name and in concert with the Lady Berthe de Châteauguay my spouse to treat of the marriage of the Lady Agnès de Châteauguay my daughter with . . ."

There being no name supplied, and the space in-blank, I extemporised.

". . . M. le vicomte Neiret, captain of vessel, to sign with the said Lady my wife the contract of marriage and represent me at the celebration of the marriage of my said daughter, promising to ratify what shall be decided and signed by the said General and my said wife; and in particular, that there should be conveyed to the said Lady Agnès my daughter the lands known as the Fish Trap, comprising twelve arpents of river frontage and all of the backwood as far as the Portage, with rights of justice and revenue, fur, feather and fin, for the enjoyment of my said daughter and her posterity in fee simple and perpetual modifying only the homage each New Year's Day of one barrel of best Armagnac."

The guests clapped their hands, as at the theatre.

Mlle Agnès was mobbed by her friends among whom, I regret to say, M. Neiret's officers intermingled.

I said: "With your permission, mademoiselle, I shall build you a cabin on your lands for your return."

I did not want M. le comte de Châteauguay to legat the lands a second time, and a third, and a fourth.

"Do you have children, M. Neilson?"

"I have a daughter of your age and a young son. It would please me more than I can say if you should be friends."

"As you command."

"And now, with your permission again, I shall find myself a violine and play a danse from my old country. The steps are not easy, and there is sometimes confusion. You and M. Neiret shall start the dance but, perhaps, not . . ."

Mlle Agnès nodded. She was not the blushing sort. By good fortune or prudent design, M. Neiret blushed for two.

XL

High tide the next day was at noon. The whole city turned out, lining the street down from the High Town, as the bridal pair walked down in a blizzard of flowers and ribalderies. I could taste on my tongue their sorrow. It was as if all that was good and young and sweet was leaving Canada, and nothing remained but to wait for the end.

The ship's sailors formed a double-hedge on the dock and piped the marrieds aboard the launch with their whistles. I watched from M. Le Ber's window in the Low Town, while he scoured Mme Neilson's bill for faults. (In reality, he was delighted to have such a good debtor in the old country, should matters go ill in the new.) I broke the crowd into halves, then quarters, then eighths: looking always for a man, now approaching the middle age, gaily dressed and conscious of the eyes of all.

Once *Junon* was just a crum on the eastern horizon, and the sad crowd dispersed, I made my way to Mme de Châteauguay's house. In the lane before the door was a bustle while, up the first pair, tradesmen were carrying off crocks and hutches. Someone had thrown the yellow flowers down and taken the vase.

Mme la comtesse must have gone aboard in the night. How could M. Neiret have refused to carry her? I own I swore at her, and called her selfish and meddlesome.

I pulled myself together. The lady did not know I needed the rival's name. I sensed that she had borne the life of a forest-widow only for her daughter's sake. Now she had done her duty, she would follow M. Neiret's star to ease and honour.

I sat down amid the dirt and said aloud:

"I need you, Huntsman Duclos."

XLI

In Canada, there is a season at the back end of the year of long, bright days with in the air just a premonition of winter. Having marked the bounds of Mme Agnès' lands with cairns, I began excavating the cellar-hole and laying the stone hearth. The Hurons made fun of me for toiling away like a woman. I had not known, until I saw them ape me, how much I halted in walking. They laughed as the Olympian Gods once laughed at limping Hephaestus.

Since I took no offence, a man who had been at Carillon became ashamed and upbraided the others and soon they were hauling the field-stones for me to sort and square. The hearth was finished in a day, and the timbers for the walls and floor the next. As I was laying reeds on the roof, I saw back fins moving upstream, like the salmon in the upper Tweed. I was sure it was the same brave creature that had elected to turn west rather than east for sweet water in which to spawn her young.

The Hurons thought little of my forest rod and running-line, preferring to deploy a species of trident in the river-mouth, but seeing that I had some success, and loving novelty, they adopted the Scottish system, and were soon more adroit angle-men than I am. The nails in overplus bent into capital hooks, which the men decorated, *ad libitum*, with deer-fur off the thorns or the feathers of grouse or woodcock. We made a sight, standing in echelon chest-deep in the tumbling stream, our lines a-curl in the air above our heads; then feasting by the fire in the long twilight before the finished house, dazed by tobacco, while flocks of wild geese clattered about our heads. The ladies salted and smoked fish enough to last Jeune Lorette the whole winter. We concerted that if we were still seeing the sun, we would return next fall for the salmon, and make any necessary reparations to the Cabane de Madame.

XLII

For a man who could lie in straw, I lived high that fall at Québec. I had, in my time, eaten a stable of horses but never served with such ceremonial. Wisking away the plate cover, my steward would murmur a culinary paternoster: *Filet de cheval à la broche avec une poivrade bien liée.* Or *Cheval à la mode.* My table-guests, and I had many, plunged in and surfaced centaurs. After dinner, I turned them out to grass in the first-pair back and picked up my business.

To vary my nourishment, and to pursue my inquiry, I accepted every invitation to dine out. I told M. Bigot that

I thought it my duty to support the moral of the better classes, and to stamp out any spirit of defeatism. For all the reduced rations and public distress, the upper town was a whirl of dances and masques.

What I misliked was the rage for gaming, at the Intendance and also at Mme Péan. Whole fortunes vanished overnight. Since, in the two great and primordial divisions of pleasure at public Assemblies, I had ever been herded with the musicians rather than the gamesters, I had gained no taste for play, but rather the contrary, and I forbade my officers to have any part in it. Some of the younger men may have obeyed me. Yet worse was the speculation in every species of money and security, even among the common soldiers, which turned the camps into a boreal rue Quincampoix. Since the habitants hoarded their coin, and there was no press to print a paper-money, the chief circulating medium was old playing-cards, signed and given a face-value by M. Vaudreuil or M. Bigot. When I received from a merchant in settlement one of my own orders on the commissary, at a 40 per centum discount, I all but knocked off the worthy lady's hat.

As it got about that I could touch keys and scratch strings, I was in request. M. Montcalm came up from Mont-Réal in mid-December to enjoy the entertainments. I suspect he hoped that his handsome person and military victories might cause one of the ladies in M. Bigot's circle to show him favour. M. and Mme Vaudreuil were incessantly expected. Then the snow came down in a heap and the stone city of Québec slept like a bear. In all my bowing and tinkling in smoky rooms, I found not a trace of M. Luynes. The rackets or snow-shoes I used were an agony to my legs. As I made my rounds at night, the guards on the rampart saluted, and the ice tinkled down from their moustaches. In the crystal air, I could hear trees splitting from the frost with the sound of a pistol shot, or the sad mewing of a lynx on the far side of the river.

On the morning of Christmas, I found at my lodging a packet, without address or signature. It contained an old circular letter, written by the Superior of the Order of Saint Ursula at Paris, and comprising excerpts from the annual reports of the Ursuline houses in France and overseas for the year 1752. The report from New-Orléans included an account of the abduction by violence of one of the boarders, Doña Ana Herrera de Revilla de Campo. Mme de Saint-Pierre had done some searches for me. This assistance, from beyond the grille of the parloir, of a lady who had withdrawn from the world and its entanglements fifty years before, greatly encouraged me.

XLIII

At New Year, I called to pay my respects to M. and Mme Vaudreuil, lately arrived by the frozen river from Mont-Réal, at the house of the adjutant, M. Péan. There was a jumbled heap of slades and snow-shoes at the porte-cochère. The house was a-blaze with fires. Supper was laid in one room, musicians in another, and tables for cards in a third. In the play-room, a gentleman in a blue velvet justicoat lounged over a gaming table in a knot of ladies.

"Paroli!"

"Sept-et-le-va!"

"Mme Vaudreuil, will you be so kind as to tell me the name of that gentleman holding the faro bank?"

"He is M. le comte d'Evreux who was with His Excellency at New-Orléans. A favourite of the ladies. Am I to present him?"

"Thank you, madame. I shall introduce myself."

I stood in the doorway of the card-room. A Pani servant brought me a glass of wine, but I did not take it.

The blue-velvet gentleman smiled at me. "Will you play, sir, or do you prefer to stare?"

"Neither, M. Evreux. I shall call on you tomorrow at eight of the morning. Have the goodness to be ready."

The music halted in mid-beat. You might have heard a wall-louse sneeze. M. Vaudreuil was at my shoulder.

"Go to your lodging, General Neilson, and there await my order."

From the other shoulder, M. Montcalm said: "Go now, William."

"That I shall do, gentlemen, but only after I have fought this man as I have sworn to do. And I shall fight any man or woman who comes between us."

The ladies scuttled from the table. M. Evreux sneered at me down the green cloth.

"I do not know you, sir, and I will not."

"But I know you, sir. Come now, M. Evreux, you are young and I am old and lame. We shall fight by torchlight. That will give the edge to young eyes. If you prevail, then none in Canada shall know the cause of our quarrel and I shall be damned in all men's judgment. If you will not fight, I shall state my grievance here and you shall die but not at my hand, for every gentleman will dagger you and every lady dip her handkin in your blood. Heavens, sir, is that not mortal insult enough?"

"Bah! I must deal with this madman."

I saw in M. Bigot's eye that he knew the cause of our quarrel, and that cause was Mlle Bouchard. His sole concern was to protect himself. The solution was as I had presented it: M. Luynes would kill me and then he would see to M. Luynes at his convenience.

M. Vaudreuil said: "I shall witness you, Étienne."

M. Luynes's eyes flickered and then settled.

M. Montcalm said: "And I shall stand for General Neilson. I know him to be a man of honour."

"I protest, M. le marquis. That would give the false impression of disunion in the military establishments of Canada. I know M. Vaudreuil will see a fair fight. With your permission, Mr Governor, we shall fight at the Place. We shall require lights. I shall attend you and your principal downstairs."

I turned and walked through a fog of hatred.

"Damn you, William. I needed you."

"I am sorry, M. le marquis."

There is nothing like a duel to bring out the courtier in a man. At the street-door, I waited for M. Luynes to precede me. He clattered down-stairs and, without a glance at my face, passed me. I waited for M. Vaudreuil but he was enmeshed in farewells.

Stepping outside, I felt a bitter cold in my stomach. My legs gave way under me. From my bed of snow, I could see M. Luynes making great strides in snow-shoes. Try as I might, I could not place these elements in their proper relation: the numbness in my belly, a great wish to sleep for all time and the crunch of racquets through the crust of ice. About me, the snow was turning dark. Ah! I thought. This is how it ends, not in the thunder of battle, but in a blanket of bloody snow. But, of course . . .

"Mr Neilson, what is it?"

"Your friend, sir, has pricked me."

From below, a shot burst in the clean air and, then, a second, and I knew that M. Luynes, also, was dead.

XLIV

In the infirmary of the Jesuit college, I sensed that I was in disgrace, and more than that. The lay-religious averted their eyes. Huron lads lay in relays across the door of my cell. Only M. Montcalm sent each day to inquire after my recovery, and then honoured me with a visit.

M. le marquis de Montcalm looked about the bare cell with approval. He appeared not overly distressed that I had been humbled. My credit with the nations, though due in whole to the friendship of the late Lord Powattamie and the generosity of Mme Neilson, was not to the taste of all the officers of old France; or, perhaps, it was my good standing with the ladies of Québec. A chair was brought for him, and a bear-skin for his feet against the cold. He said:

"I am not a little surprised, William, that my cousin did not petition His Majesty for a patent of nobility for you."

"I am, sir, Earl of Biggar in the County of Lanark in Scotland by the favour of King James and, in the nobility of Persia, Jagar ol-Soltan, or Liver of the Sovereign. Liver, in the particular sense of that country, means not the vital organ but something like 'favourite' or 'pet'."

"I see," M. Montcalm said. "Beside such dignities, a French nobility is but a bagatelle." He leaned forward to the bed-head. "It is said that your challenge was simply a bait to draw M. Evreux into an ambush of assassins. It is said he stabbed you in desperate self-defence."

"What does M. Bigot say?"

"Nothing to deny it."

"Shall you write, M. le marquis, to your cousin by the first vessel to leave the river?"

M. Montcalm looked at me as if I were a madman. Then he roared with laughter.

"But you will tiff, William, and I shall take her part!"

"I am used to obeying her. The lady worked a miracle in the île de France and île Bourbon, and will do so here."

I sensed that M. Montcalm, chafing under his subordination to M. Vaudreuil, was not anxious to submit to the dominion of his cousin.

"William, now is not the time nor Canada the place for

an experiment in feminine government. All I can do is warn you of what awaits outside these sanctified walls."

"Thank you, sir."

At the door, he turned and said in a low voice: "I believe you and I shall not see dear France again. I am sorry, William."

"Do not be. I would not have missed this place for a second lifetime."

That was not true in every degree. There were moments in my cell when I missed the warmth of my son in my arms fit to weep. Sometimes, and especially in the snow-light of the morning, I sensed Jeanne in the room with me, insubstantial, familiar to me as my own face in a looking-glass, but of a different form and will, and for that reason dear beyond anything of my own. I wished that I would live to see Mlle de Joyeuse married to M. Duclos and reconciled with her god-mother.

XLV

"Father, will you hear my confession, for I have sinned?"

"Yes, my son. When was your last confession?"

"I do not recollect having made a confession, as such."

"Then, you have much to confess."

"In the year 'Forty-seven, I was living in France as a guest of the lady who is now my wife. In those days, I was an adherent of the Pretended Reformed Religion, which was the cult of my fathers and much of my homeland."

"That was a grave sin, my son."

"Can we not, Reverend Father, pile up the sins and deal with them in a heap?"

"As you prefer, my son."

"My lady was dying of the small pox, which I was able to cure through a course of variolation I had seen practised in the Indies."

"Did you employ the Turkish or the Chinese system?"

"Father Laval, might we not defer philosophical questions to a less solemn occasion?"

"As you wish, my son."

"During the illness of their mistress, the house and outdoors servants became disaffected and neighbours sought to appropriate portions of her estate. With God's help, the lady recovered. Being a person of much scientific knowledge, she resolved to perform an inoculation against the small pox of both her servants and her tenants, comprising some four hundred and sixty men, women and children. Her people feared such a novel treatment, which had at that time not been tried in Mother France. A servant-girl, a foundling from the Hôtel-Dieu of Orléans, not ten years of age, stepped forward for the surgical treatment and shamed her elders. My lady, who had despaired that God would give her a child of her body, was touched to the heart by the child's bravery and loyalty, took her into her apartments and poured on her that maternal love that had but been waiting for an object. My lady taught the child to read and write and relieved her of the hard duties that had been her lot. Nobody in the district doubted but that my lady would adopt the child, who was named Marie-Ange de La Contrition, as her heiress."

"Go on, my son."

"I said that the child had been relieved of her duties, but one remained. In my lady's woods, there lived alone in a tumbled bothy the ancient nurris of her father, who would admit nobody but the little foundling. One day in April of 1747, at about one hour after noon, the lass was carrying the dame's dinner down one of the woodland rides, when she was accosted by a richly dressed young man, who gave her a bunch of primeveres . . ."

"Communis or officinalis?"

"Communis. The gentleman rode on, but the child was frightened out of her senses. When informed of this, my lady ordered her hunt servants to make a careful investigation. They found evidence that two further men had been waiting in ambush by the ride. With difficulty, they persuaded my lady to have the lass continue in her ordinair routine. Six days later, at the same hour and in the same place, they caught the two men, poor old soldiers, who gave to my lady the name of the well-dressed gentleman."

"Did you mistreat the men?"

"Yes."

"That was a grave sin, my son, and also tainted their evidence."

"I recognise that, Reverend Father."

"Continue, my son."

"The night of the men's confession, a showy sort of gentleman, M. le comte de Luynes, my lady's nephew or, to be precise, cousin german at one remove, called at her house. Though he did not see me, I had a good sight of him in the torchlight. A little later, my lady told me that she had exiled him to Louisiana with letters of recommendation to M. Vaudreuil. I demurred, saying that I would challenge M. Luynes, but was overruled. For years, we had no word of the gentleman. M. Vaudreuil, in replying from New Orléans to my lady's letters, said no such person as M. Luynes had come into the territory. It was only when I came here after the fight at Carillon and heard of the death of Mlle Bouchard that I remembered him. Against the wishes, even the orders of M. Bigot, I inquired into the matter. I also learned from an immaculate source that a young girl, of a good family of Cuba, had been abducted and done to death at New Orléans in 'Fifty-two. I waited on Mme Bouchard, but she had nothing to report of her daughter's doings, except that beside her lifeless body at the foot of the Falls of Montmorency was a bouquet of yellow flowers."

I drew breath. "Dear Reverend Father, the rest you know. You may also understand, from my discourse, why at the dinner at the house of Mme la comtesse de Chateauguay, when I saw the yellow wild-flowers on the mantle, I pressed marriage on the young people with such uncalled-for and boorish insistence."

"They did not appear so greatly averse to passing their lives together in Christian marriage."

"Ah! You thought that. I had a notion it was so. Weel, you were good enough to bless them and afterwards, you will recollect, we passed to the grave of poor Mlle Bouchard where was laid—

"A spray of ciliata."

"Yes, father. I thought you had not remarked it. And so we come to the New Year's gala at the Intendance, where I challenged M. Evreux, whom I knew to be M. Luynes *sub falso nomine*, and received from him the wound that you were so kind as to tend."

Father Laval closed his eyes. Opening them, he said:

"There is nothing here, my son, that would convince an impartial spectator, let alone the omniscient God, of M. Evreux's crime. There is no such branch of learning as forensic botany. What happened that night in the snow is known to God. What concerns us is the salvation of your soul, how far-fetched so ever that might appear. Did you not act in a spirit of hatred or of avarice, which are deadly sins? Had you expectations of your lady's succession in preference to M. Luynes?"

"I had renounced them. Her legatees were the foundling, known as Mlle de Joyeuse, and our son, the Chevalier Neilson."

"Do you know who killed M. Evreux?"

"No."

"Do you have any suspicions?"

"I can only surmise that the assassins were relations of Mlle Bouchard, or of Doña Ana de Revilla in New-Orléans."

"*Pluralitas non est ponenda sine necessitate.*"

Possibilities should not be multiplied beyond need.

"I am sure, father."

"What about relations of the foundling, now called Mlle de Joyeuse?"

"She has no relations here but I."

"Then you alone are suspect. Did you employ confederates to kill M. de Luynes?"

"No."

Father Laval paused and then took on another subject. "Have you attended Mass?"

"I don't believe so, father. Possibly, at Venice, in the Basilica of Saint Mark, at the Feast of the Ascension in 'Forty-seven."

"So your faith is only for show or for preferment in His Majesty's service."

"No, no, father. I sincerely wished to please my lady. I knew she would not marry me unless I were a Catholic."

"William, that is not adequate ground!"

I had an inspiration. "I have read the Holy Bible twice in its entirety in Latin." I added, for the sake of candour: "In prison."

"Were you often in prison, my son?"

"More than I would have chosen."

"Have you killed?"

"Yes, father."

"How many?"

"One hundred and ninety-two men and boys."

"In battle?"

"Yes, father. They were the Irish men that through my vanity and pride I led to death in the fight in Scotland."

"That is a sin only if it was your intention."

"Father, it is not especially hard to command men in battle, just so long as one keeps one's mental concentration. I gave way to elation and self-content. That, not the death of M. Luynes, or my defective religious observances, is the sin that damns me to Hell."

"Have you asked God's forgiveness?"

"I do not want forgiveness."

"Are you sure of that, my son?"

Something occurred to me then, such as in my life I had never known. It was as if the dam that held back my sorrow had started to buckle and crack and then, all at once, burst. It was as if I were baptised in my tears.

"Are you sure of that, my son?"

"No."

"Shall you pray to God for forgiveness?"

"Yes."

"What do you know of Jansenius?"

"I am not acquainted with the gentleman."

"Really, William, you are so sinful and ignorant I do not know where to begin. I have met men running through the woods at Stinkards' Bay who know more of the Catholic religion. Our Reverend Bishop declares that our scourges are merited and just punishment for our sins. Thank the Lord that he has no knowledge of your irreligion and shall not have.

"There is no question of absolution. Your penance is thus. You are to read your catechism and be prepared to be tested. You are to attend Mass each morning except when on campaign. On return, you shall make up the deficit by supernumerary masses. You are to find the killer of M. Luynes. You are to write me a report on the inoculation against small-pox conducted at your lady's house *in terra Sabulonia*, *anno* 1747."

"I have it with me."

"That shall suffice for your fourth penance."

I believe that the confessional is private and sacrosanct. None the less, Révérend Père Laval called on Mme Bouchard in the snow and that lady was seen at Mass in better spirits than she had been since the death of her child.

When quizzed on the matter, Mme Bouchard would only say: "Our Lady answered my prayer."

The tale took wind and, after a time, I was re-admitted into the good society of Québec. Mme Péan was my protectress, and as pretty, clever and kind a lady as one could hope to meet. It was an agreeable society, with few privileges to insist upon, hardy and embued with a spirit of liberty that came (I think) with the woods and the wind. The women were better lettered than the men, by reason of the Ursuline board-school, and were both gallant and chaste, which is the best society for a married man far from home. Mme Péan told me that, at first, they had thought me just another enraged Scotchman, friend only to the woods and the wild men; but I had improved.

Gentlemen and ladies, they had embraced M. Montcalm's system of European war. Bourgeois, munitioners, merchants, voyageurs, bishops, curates, Jesuits, Récollets instructed me in tactics and explained to me strategics. Every gentleman was a Saxe and every lady a Turenne.

XLVI

The winter afternoons I passed at Jeune Lorette, attempting to master the native jargon. Richard, my dominie, had the singular fault of never once admitting in anything to ignorance. If he did not know something, he invented it. My evenings I passed in my lodging, bundled by the stove, engaged in a scheme I had long projected, and for which I had for years been gathering materials, which was to write the history of my life with you, Jeanne de Joyeuse. If I have been false in my recollection of events, I have been true to my sentiments, which the heart retains with complete precision and cannot be corrupted or abated. Do with these pages as you please. Since my confession to Father Laval a sort of lightness of heart has come to me. If God pardons me, so shall my Irish men. I no longer fear dying. Rather, out of my usual parsimony, I have resolved to die but once.

With the thaw, the whole country became a puddle. The hills roared with torrents, and the ice on the river boomed and crackled. Outside, there were bursts of warmth as tokens of midsummer. To exercise the native men after the long winter, and to clear out any temporarie residents, animal and human, we crossed over the river to Mlle Agnès' lands to draw the sugar from her érables or sweet-maple trees. I could see from the puffs of smoke above the tree-tops that the men were making rum for sale in the Lower Town. I turned a blind eye.

I had long despaired of the Outagamie and thanked Providence that I had not accepted the two young lads as hostages. On our return in good fettle from the south side, we found a party of that nation, worn out and hungry from the tramp down from the High Country, and very much depleted in strength. The rougeole or meazles had killed or made invalids of a quarter of the nation. I had them at once removed to the île d'Orléans, to serve out a quarantine. Since I was sure they had been exposed to the scourge in the camp at Carillon, I promised to cover the dead with presents, just as if they had fallen in battle, which appeared to render their isolation more acceptable.

Alas! The Mission Hurons came to me and all but accused me of favourising. The Outagamie chief, also addressed as Powattamie since the name, like Caesar, attached to the dignity not the individual, was but twenty years old, strong and handsome and, like many new-appointed men, excessively susceptible in the matter of his dignity. I called a conference and explained, as best as I might, that across the water it was the practice, in a place under siege, to suspend all quarrels and disputes over precedence until the end of the emergency might permit their resolution through an exchange of gifts or trial of arms. After a time, that was found reasonable.

I had brought from La Ferté two wide necklaces or belts of sea-shells of the very finest American art that had been at the castle, much cherished by Mme Neilson, since the time of her grandfather, Keeper of the Seals under Louis the Great. They had been sent from Mont-Réal by M. le marquis de Frontenac, then Governor General. Mme Neilson had an idea they had served to commemorate or, in some sense beyond our understanding, notarise some great event or diplomatic treaty. A novice in American politics, I had been reluctant to show them, lest they carry some evil recollection from the past, but it was now or never. The chiefs showed no surprise, far less enthusiasm, but I remarked that they did not touch or even approach those mysterious objects. I proposed that, for the duration of the campaign, and by the favour of Bishop Pontbriand, the belts should be exposed above the High Altar in the Cathedral. That was approved.

That same day, a deputation of Abénaquie, from south of the river, who were as pinched with hunger as everybody else, arrived below the walls and proposed that they smoke the pipe, sing the war song and put some flesh on their ribs. I now could dispose of a force of some eight hundred effective men. It was a modest strength for a general officer of France to direct, and all the more in that I could not achieve any co-operation between the different nations that would allow me to concentrate the whole force. The chiefs might accept suggestions from me but not from one another. I thanked Providence that, in six years imprisonment in the castle of the Bastille, I had learned patience.

How was I to feed them? The hunger of the winter was now famine. M. Bigot had reduced the daily ration to just four ounces of bread. The little wheat was mixed with oats and pease so it was as black as the habit of the Ursulines. Squads of women besieged the Intendance and my hangar at Jeune Lorette, which I opened to all till it was bare.

Out in the country, the King's soldiers were quartered on the habitants who, having campaigned all summer without pay, could barely support their families, could not feed their animals and had not sown their lands. Oxen were taken out of the plough to be slaughtered and salted. Only cavalry horses were spared the butcher's knife. The Hurons killed their dogs.

I feared I would have to send the Outagamie back to the High Country and they would not be pleased.

XLVII

The boldest wager on the first ship of spring was for May 10th. On the 8th, word came up that an armed flûte, *Le Dromadaire*, Captain Drummond commanding, was in the road.

She looked as if she had been in a fight. I was much engaged, and did not join the mob at the dock.

I was tying up the threads of business when I looked up. Before me stood a dazed old salt. I rose.

"I am right pleased to see you, Mr Drummond."

"And I ye, Gen'l Neilson." The mariner's single eye played like a sunbeam over my red riband and gold galloon. "Didna your faither have the roup in the Cowget of Edinbro?"

"Aye, and wasna Our Saviour's daddie a joiner-bodie

from Galilee-side? We Scots are ay thrassing the upmaist thrissels."

Captain Drummond looked resentful.

"Come now, Mr Drummond, those are mere plaisanteries. Have you not news of my lady?"

"Aye, Willie. Letters I have from Her Leddyship, brought a-board by Her Leddyship hersel. With your fine laddie."

I broke the seal. The letter was *en clair.* There was no date, address or subscription and I thought, at first, that a first page was missing:

It was the evening of the day I received the terms from the gentlemen at Warsaw. She came to me, bare-foot, and knelt down and asked if she might be released from my service, taking only a dress and cap such as she had brought with her from the Hospital. I cried that she was not my servant, but my beloved daughter, my heart, my life, my posterity. If Poland were not to her taste, I would break off the treaty with Warsaw, and pay the indemnity, but marry she must within her rank, else have no hope of happiness, usefulness or regard. In tears and kisses we parted, I thought, friends.

Yet, all night I could not sleep. Peeping into her room

at dawn, I found it empty and her bed cold. Later in the morning, Mme Dalouhe brought news that M. Duclos was nowhere to be found.

I raged at you. Why had not Mr Neilson halted me in my mad career? Then I remembered that every day you tried to discourage me and halt the Modena marriage, and would surely have opposed Poland and Lithuania with augmented vigour. I knew that I was your inferior in most affairs, but not in this. As in all things all my wretched life, I was deceived.

I have no anger for M. Duclos. He had risked his life for Mlle de Joyeuse. I had planned that, once you and I were gone, he would be her right hand as Mme Dalouhe would be her left. Yet such was my pride and ignorance, I never considered for a moment that they might like. And so, dearest friend, a single fault wipes out whatever good I have done in the world and turns it all into evil.

How often I took up my pen to write to you of my disaster! The occasion of a merchant ship ready to sail from Brest, which counted on reaching the entrance to the Saint-Laurent before the ice was set, gave me the opportunity but I had not the courage to seize it. I feared that you would straightaway return, risk your life and honour and the safety of Canada to make the traverse in winter, and all to console a vain, foolish and meddlesome old woman. Also, I prayed that by the spring I might have intelligence of Marie-Ange. God has decreed otherwise.

The news of Carillon came like a thunder-clap out of a blue sky. It is said they rang the bells of the cathedral of Our Lady at Paris, and I feared the village belfries here would shake to rubble. (We are not so rich in military heroes, that we did not at once claim you as a Solognote.) My son and I drank in every item: your arrival with the native men at the height of battle, the fight at the rampart, and the capture of brave Mr Harris. Gentlemen were calling to their friends across the street: "Is that you, William? Do you speak French?" Old military men were saying that now that M. Montcalm has Mr Neilson by his side, he cannot fail to hold the colony.

The spirit did not last. The report of the loss of Louisbourg threw the people back into their dejection. At the castle of Chambord, I heard a gentleman say that Canada had never earned a sou, and we would need to give her up to preserve our advantages in Europe. At all costs, we must keep the sugar islands. It was as much as I could do to keep my self-control.

With the sale of the Désert, I have paid off all the bankers' advances, but have taken an additional two millions from M. Martin at Geneva, for reasons I shall here explain.

I have been at the Palace of Versailles, where I waited on the Secretary of the Marine, M. Berryer. He kept me in antechambers and, as there was no bed at the palace, I had to bide out two nights in a cabaret. I was so disordered from lying out of my bed that I made but a poor showing in my interview. When M. Berryer at last received me, he treated Canada with levity. When the house is on fire, he said in a laugh, one does not rush to save the stables. This sally got wind and was thought most spirited. I had only to appear for people to whisper behind their hands. Cannot they see that, without Canada, there will be no France or at least no royal France!

There are women at this Court so withdrawn into their beauty that rather than ruffle or disturb it they say and do nothing. One passes through an enfilade of petrified goddesses. I thank God that my disobedience in the matter of your reading in prison caused my father to withdraw me from Court. Anyway, M. le duc thought little of the Capets.

I was dressed to depart, and waiting for my coach to be brought up, when Mme la marquise de Pompadour summoned me, and bade me lodge with her in her apartment. We worked together three mornings and supped head-to-head. She is a woman of sense whom you must henceforth regard as the first minister of France. It is her interest that does what little is done. She is younger than I am, more clever and much prettier, but not in the best of health. We concerted that, if I engaged to spend two millions on the colony this winter, she would match that sum from her fortune. The fate of Canada now depends on a shining paladin at one side of the Great Water, and at the other on two ladies of indifferent moral character.

Mme de Pompadour said on parting that if you and M. Montcalm succeed and hold Canada until the peace, she shall ask the King to make you marshals of France. I replied that neither you nor, as far as I was aware, M. Montcalm had any concern for such things; to which she repliqued, with grace, that the King would be so much more the ready to honour you.

We have been at Dunkerque, Bayonne, Lorient, Nantes and Saint-Malo, young William and I. At Dunkerque, M. Douvry demanded 2,000 francs for every ton of freight, more than twice what the other armateurs are asking, and four times the rate before the present war. Alas! I am not rich enough for M. Douvry. By a patent that he asked me to read for him, he is vicomte de Terre-Neuve, a pretty nobility that suits him entirely.

At Lorient, M. Béranger was lapped in tobacco and ease, but recommended his wife's son, M. Neiret, who has twice sailed the Saint-Laurent, which is difficult by reason of the shoals and fogs and the want of capable pilots. Under the suggestion of my friend at Court, the Secretary of Marine granted M. Neiret furlough. Captain Neiret will command the Junon, *and one of your countrymen, Mr Drummond, the* Dromadaire. *M. Neiret is the handsomest man I ever saw except you and Mr Law, Mr Drummond less so, but a worthy man.*

It was the Chevalier who proposed we reduce the canons from twelve pounds to eight, which will leave twenty tons in overplus for supply. M. Neiret believes that speed and sailorship, and not armament, will bring him through the English blockade. My fear is rather that the sea-nymphs will espy him and drag him down into the deeps for their several pleasure.

The cargo, which has been inspected by my son, consists of wine, eau de vie, dried fruits, twelve hundred quarts of wheat-flour, biscuit, rice, salted beef, bacon, pease, tobacco, powder, lead-shot, Tulle muskets, Normandie blankets, red and blue Limburg cloth, woollen stockings, Holland linen and items for trade or presents for the nations of as good quality as comes from New England. I could find no assurance for a prime less than 75 per cent of the value of bottom and cargo, and thus have entrusted the vessels to God and the skill of their pilots and captains.

I have resolved not to send coin which is anyway all but impossible to procure and would only be hidden away by the habitants or pass into the English colonies. Instead, I shall accept and pay at sight bills of exchange on Paris for the entire playing-card money of Canada sent with the last vessel to sail for France in the autumn, provided each bill is countersigned by you or M. Montcalm. Pardon me for giving you the labour, but it is of the first importance for the credit of both cards and bills. Mlle de Joyeuse (whose plan this was) believed that, since my credit is better than that of the Department of Marine, the card money will rise in value or the price of provisions in Canada will fall, being the same thing. I understand that will be a charge of a further million this year and possibly for several years but, as my darling said, you made them rich with your canal and it is the least she could do for you and for our beloved France.

M. Martin's intention through his ready accommodation is to gain control of the canal, and convert it into a toll-way, and that may yet come about. It may be that I shall need to sell both the hôtel in the rue Varenne and La

Ferté-Joyeuse. I promise you that I shall live, alone and naked, in the woods rather than suffer you, your men or your autochthonous allies to want for anything.

I have insisted to both captains in the strictest terms that the provisions of war and mouth belong not to the King but to you and are to be delivered not to the King's Intendant, the Society, the general munitioner or the store-houses of Québec but only to your order. Else those leeches will hide them to keep up prices or, even, I believe, destroy them. In the course of my work with Mme de Pompadour, I was shown trade correspondence that made me weep not just for Canada but for all France.

Now I am occupied, I am less frightened, and the Chevalier is a hero in these difficulties. He has come from out of his sister's shadow and is as good a son as any mother could wish. To see him discoursing amid the smokey old mariners, like Our Lord in the temple! He knows why Marie-Ange has gone and, I believe, whither, but I cannot bear to make him betray her confidence. He says only that she told him: "I shall bring no dishonour on Maman." In my torment of shame and rage and blasphemy, without husband, daughter and fortune, God has left me a consolation which I do not deserve. Mme Plaie lets fall that she, too, knows the where and why of Mlle de Joyeuse, but only to riot in my fear and grief. As they say here, where the Devil himself cannot go, he sends an old woman.

I was told at the Palace that M. le comte de Luynes is dead, shot by a common soldier of La Reine battalion, and I am glad.

Though I am not with you to share your privations, you are never out of my thoughts. My son has confided to me that he has your permission to join you as ensign at his fourteenth birthday. I ask that I may travel with him oversea, so we shall live and die together.

I believe that God will bring us together, and I shall once more see you and Mlle de Joyeuse.

PS You will pardon me in that I have sent the sable tails to Mme la duchesse de Bourbon with your duty. Please send us no more, beautiful as they are. Let the brave animals live.

"Come, Mr Drummond. Let us dine."

As we set off, I called my aide-de-camp to bring me the strength of La Reine battalion, preliminary to an inspection tomorrow at first call.

XLVIII

On the 10th, a frigate came in bringing M. Bougainville, showing the badge of colonel and the ribbon of Saint-Louis, but leading just four hundred unhappy recruits. When he presented the orders from the Court, the ulterior purpose of his mission to Versailles became evident. M. Montcalm was promoted lieutenant-general, and now outranked M. Vaudreuil, a captain of vessel. The surprise at this revolution in the military command of Canada was overtaken, a few days later, by the arrival of M. Cadet's transports from Bordeaux, numbering twenty-two laden vessels. If we are to be beaten by the English, it will not be for want of nourishment.

On May 23rd, word was brought me that two merchant captains had seen up to ten sail at Saint Barnabé downstream. The progress of the English fleet up-river was slow, and it was fully a month before it reached the city. None the less, it made a magnificent sight, twenty ships of war and twice that force in transports, spread out across the entire river-basin. Mr Wolfe, the English commander, made camp at the west end of the île d'Orléans, erected a block-house on the north shore beyond the Falls and placed cannon on the heights opposite the city, which began casting shot with no particular purpose into the town.

We had spent the spring months making a strong fortification of the whole north coast as far as the Falls, while the narrows and high cliffs upstream of the town made any landing there most perilous. The campaigning season was already well advanced. It was for Mr Wolfe to act and M. Montcalm to observe.

There is nothing so dispiriting to a troop than being required to await without movement the slow advance of a superior enemy. To occupy the men, and to give young Powattamie his first command in battle, I proposed a night raid on the English pickets at their camp beyond the Falls. The purpose, I informed M. Montcalm, was to gather intelligence of the English dispositions.

I had hoped to take part in the action but M. Powattamie rewarded my confidence by excluding me, without any of the common native diplomacy, as being slow, timorous and noisy. I heard that the men crossed at a ford high up the Montmorency River, came amid the English pickets and, at the shriek of a night-owl, struck their matches. No shot was fired, but in the pandemonium, I fear many of the English lads went into the water and drowned.

The moral effect of the night action on the men was all I could have wished. True, the men had not yet scalps to carry back to their home country. They were rewarded with the choice of Mr Drummond's supply, the brightest muskets, the richest coverings and the sweetest tobacco. Having won his spurs and been established in his authority, young Powattamie became a little less unamiable. Like his great predecessor and namesake, he cared not for brandy and his men, for the most part, followed his example.

The native men brought back six captives including a young lieutenant who was well supplied with flesh. He did not appreciate the Huron ladies pinching his legs and hams as if deliberating how those cuts might be dressed for the table. I told him that his captors were, in the main, pious Roman Catholics and had been so for a century, but my assurance was of small comfort. It required very little questioning on my part to acquire a good notion of the English plan of battle. It was nothing less than an assault from the water on our position on the north shore at Beauport, its strongest place, with a flanking action from across the Montmorency. By such means, M. Montcalm would be forced into battle.

M. le chevalier de Lévis could not at first believe that the English would attempt a landing so reckless, but, excellent officer that he was, established a strong line in the houses and gardens behind our redoubts.

The fight, when it came on July 31st, was a horrid

shambles. As often occurs in co-operation of land and water, the English soldiers and sailors were at cross-purposes. The naval men sent in two colliers, bristling with cannon, but they ran aground and could not bring their guns to bear on our lines. As for the landing-crafts, the naval officers had misjudged the tide and the poor English grenadiers had to cram for six hours in the hot sun, annoyed by our fire, until the tide should recede. Beyond the Falls, General Townshend was also waiting for the water to drop so he could ford the river and attack our left. All the while, black clouds were gathering overhead.

There are engagements in which brave soldiers may redeem the errors of their commanders. This fight was not among such. The English grenadiers rushed up from the shore with their bayonets fixed. The native men, better supplied with lead-shot by Mme Neilson's bounty than our regulars or militia, kept up from the cover of the houses a keen fire and forced the Englishmen to withdraw, in good order, taking (thank God) most of their wounded brothers. A second English line had formed on the shore, and might have suffered the same fate as that of the first, had not the storm broken, turned the steep ground into mud and ruined their powder. In danger of being cut off, Mr Townshend retired back across the Montmorency

River. The English lost some five hundred men. M. Bougainville said that one more attack like that and Mr Wolfe would have no force left to him.

On the morrow of the battle, over my objections, M. le marquis de Montcalm named me to treat with the English over the exchange of prisoners from both actions. At the inn of Saint-Anne, where the conference was set, the English delegates were led by an officer of cavalry. He looked at me and skittered back.

"I know you, sir, damn you!"

"Ah," I said, "English civilities."

I rose and extended my hand. "I am General Neilson, damn me."

"I will not touch the hand of a traitor."

"Weel, Major . . ."

". . . Chumley."

". . . shall you ask Mr Wolfe to send a gentleman less scrupulous. We hold," I looked at my paper, "eighty-seven of your officers and men. You have but six of our deserters, whom we have no special eagerness to recover."

"I demand that the French commander appoint another officer to conduct the treaty."

"Alas! Mr Chumley, you may demand nothing of M. le marquis de Montcalm until you have defeated him, which, after your misfortune yesterday, does not seem imminent.

He appointed me to treat with you because I speak a little English. Good day to you, sir."

I stood up, but something nibbled at the foot of my memory.

"Forgive me, Major Chumley, but I do not recollect our former reunion."

"In the Rebellion. On Culloden Moor."

"Ah," I said. "I am glad you came to no great harm, sir."

XLIX

Mr Wolfe began to show signs of impatience. Having learned the butcher's trade in the Highlands of Scotland in the Rebellion, he sent out parties to burn all the farms, churches and settlements on each side of the river and kill and scalp or drive off the habitants. By such severe measures, the gentleman hoped to shame Mr Montcalm into marching out for a pitched battle in which the better-schooled English forces must prevail. Mr Wolfe was disappointed. In the council of war, I proposed taking the entire native force across the river, to protect the poor habitants, harry the communication between the English camp and the artillery position across from the town, cut off stragglers, and destroy supply. My proposal was not adopted.

When a subordinate officer finds his views over-ridden, he is presented with various courses of action. He may, like Achilles, sulk in his tent, plead ill-health or such, resign his commission. He may submit to his chief's will while hoping that the superiorities of his policy must, in the elapse of time, become manifest. And he may snap to and forget the whole business. I chose the last of those courses. None the less, I was sent in the first week of August to watch for any landing by the English upstream of Québec, not so much because M. Montcalm thought that probable but to maintain the line of communication with Mont-Réal and usher me and our native allies out of his sight.

I was upriver the night of August 9th, when the English artillery at Pointe-de-Lévy bombarded the Basse-Ville to destruction. The Hurons were prodigies of valour in bringing people out of the burning houses, but could not save the stores or the church of Notre-Dame-des-Victoires. Nobody remembered that, in my project of razing the Lower Town, the church would have been left standing. Under cover of the smoke, more and more English vessels passed upstream and anchored at cap Rouge. At my request, I was reinforced with a troop of volunteer horse and a company of grenadiers. Had I . . .

I can write no more. I have driven back five assaults above the town and, the season advancing, the English may have to turn about or starve the winter in the river ice. I live each day as if it shall be my last and, though I would have wished my little family about me, I am happy.

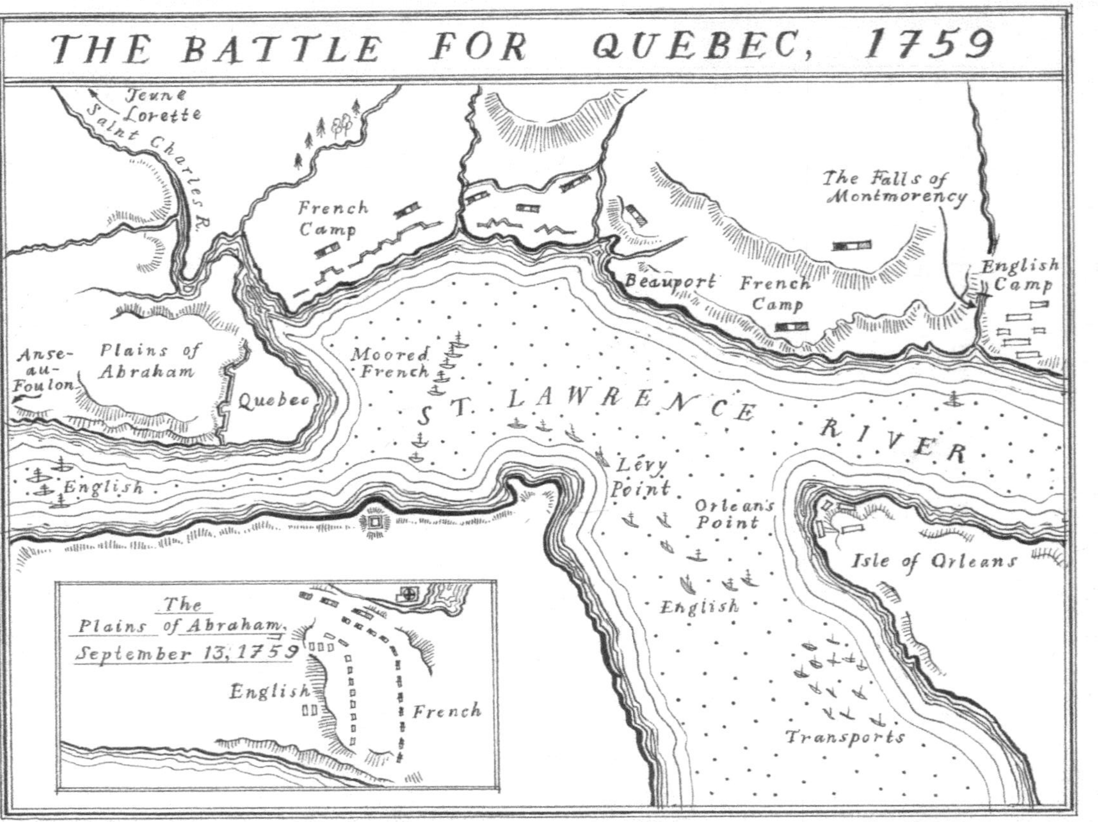
THE BATTLE FOR QUEBEC, 1759
Jeune Lorette
Saint Charles R.
French Camp
The Falls of Montmorency
English Camp
Beauport
French Camp
Anse-au-Foulon
Plains of Abraham
Quebec
Moored French
ST. LAWRENCE RIVER
English
Lévy Point
Orlean's Point
Isle of Orleans
English
Transports
The Plains of Abraham, September 13, 1759
English
French

PART 3

Our Lady of the Snows, 1760

L

The English landed in the early hours of September 13th at Anse-au-Foulon or Fuller's Cove, about one league above the town, made their way up the cliff and formed line at the place we call the Plains of Abraham. Mr Neilson, who had repelled a feint at cap Rouge, did not hear of the ascent until five of the morning, when he made haste with all his force, numbering some six hundred men in five companies of grenadiers and several bands of native men, the artillery to follow at its own pace.

It may be that M. le marquis de Montcalm wished to fight a pitched battle of European type. Certainly, the English position was as bad as it could be. Our right overlapped their left, and there was in their position no possibility of either entrenchment or retreat. I heard later M. Montcalm was in error, and should have awaited Mr

Neilson's arrival from cap Rouge; but a beaten general is always in the wrong.

Prospera omnes sibi vindicant; adversa uni imputantur.

All claim a share of victory but defeat is the fault of just one.

We were marched up from Beauport, and formed in lines of six with our backs to the town walls. I heard no order to advance, but in a moment we were moving in a mass. Men fired off their pieces long before they were in shot, then threw themselves to the ground to recharge. The English fired rolling volleys which formed a sort of wall we could not penetrate. I later heard that, in the first exchanges, both M. Montcalm and Mr Wolfe were wounded beyond hope of recovery.

In the rout of our army, M. Duclos was able to rally some of the men of our La Reine battalion, to which were added some native men and Canadians who felt it was oversoon to be giving up. In a wood by the Saint-Jean gate, we kept up a warm fire in enfilade and stopped the English seeking to seize the bridge over the Saint-Charles River. My intention was to form a junction with Mr Neilson's force, and press the English against the walls of town where we could not but be successful. As we crossed the battle-field, cannonaded by friend and foe alike, we came on the saddest scene I have ever witnessed.

The English grenadiers formed ranks to resist us, but I threw off my cap and shook down my hair, and they shrank from me as if Juno herself had descended to the battle field. I stooped under the musket barrels, with M. Duclos alone following. I found Mr Neilson in the last extremity, bleeding from the chest and mouth from ball-wounds. His eye-sockets were brimming with blood.

"Is that you, my darling?"

"We will take you to safety."

"I am on my way. Please seek out Mr Harris, who will honour you and plead your cause with your maman."

"General Harris is fallen, sir." That was the English officer.

"Ach. What a whole story that ends today! Is M. Duclos with you?"

"I am here, general."

"I would wish that you two were soon married."

"We are married, father."

"God bless you," he said. And then: "Love my boy and tell your maman . . ." and, again, "Tell your maman . . ." Then Mr Neilson coughed, and could not find a breath, and died.

We placed the hero on a litter, and Mr Stokes, the English officer, who, unlike most Englishmen, spoke really quite good French, gave us escort to the Saint-Louis gate. It would not open for us and M. Duclos and the officer commanding had words. The streets were full of running women who, when they saw the bier, set up a keening.

"My good friends, we still have the town. Have courage!"

We carried Mr Neilson to the Ursulines and I laid him in the chapel. I gave the sisters what card money I had, and wrote in their day-book an epitaph. In preparing the body for burial, the good ladies found sewn into Mr Neilson's bloody shirt a scrap of linen embroider'd with the arms of my family, and I took it away to carry to my godmother. Our condition was bad but not desperate. I reckoned we would need to resist for just ten days before the English must sail away.

In the street before the convent, M. Duclos and the native captains were engaged in a council of war. It appeared that, under the pleas of the merchants and M. Bigot, our commanders had in mind to give up the town. Thinking that poor recompense for our loss, I proposed we make our way out in which scheme M. Duclos seconded me. With a force now increased to one hundred and fifty, militia, Huron, Outagamies and some twenty of the King's soldiers, we drove through the English lines without loss, and made our way to M. le chevalier de Lévis at Montréal, harrying the English columns and taking many scalps. In the peril and exertion of that winter, and the incessant violence, I had not leisure to grieve.

While the English held the ruins of Québec, the colony was all for France. M. Lévis assembled a force and, on April 28th, 1760, at precisely the same place where we had fought in September last, drove the English back into the city and placed it under siege.

Our supplies of munitions and food were exhausted, and there was nothing to be found in the desolation all about. It was said that, without a convoy from the metropolis, the siege must be lifted. No such reinforcement came and, indeed, the first ships to enter the river were English. One might have thought that our staff officers were looking for an honourable pretext not to carry on the fight. When a nation is bent on defeat, there is a little a particular person may do to forestall or delay that defeat. M. Duclos was in the town with his intelligencers, and it was only with the utmost difficulty that I was able to bring them out.

Mr Murray, the English commander, marched and shipped his men upstream, burning everything in his way. We did what he could to hamper his operations, but by mid-summer famine drove us back on Mont-Réal. At the île Sainte-Hélène, one league downstream from the town, we learned that M. Vaudreuil had signed articles of capitulation to surrender the colony, in terms disgraceful to the honour of France and her arms. By reason of my barbarous and unwomanly conduct, I was excepted by name from the amnesty. General Amherst ordered I be handed over for summary justice. I was for making our way to the Illinois country and across the great river to found a New Canada in the west, but M. Duclos demurred, saying it was my duty to carry the ill tidings of General Neilson's death to my maman, plead for her forgiveness and console her in her loss. The native captains excused themselves, *uno animo*, from giving counsel.

I submitted, asking Mr Stokes (who had come with escort to convey me to the English camp) the grace of an half-hour to change into women's costume. In that interval, to spare poor M. Lévis, I took our band across the water and into the woods. That was the first time, I believe, that the native men of Canada fought in formation. They did very well; but M. Duclos said that they only did so to show they were able, and he would not ask them to do so again.

At the portage of the Chaudière, we took leave of our Outagamie friends, so they might reap their harvest at the Détroit. M. Duclos, with a single Abénaquie for companion, set off with snow-shoes for Boston with my bill in-blank, in the hope that my mother's credit might preponderate my crimes among the merchants of that bourg. Our people, consisting of ninety-two of the King's soldiers and one hundred and twenty-five French and indigenous men, women and children, I carried down the Saint-Jean River and encamped on the shore, where we had a hard time of it. The English had burned every farm and hamlet along the river-side, but, after some days, men and women crept like ghosts out of the trees and we did what we could for them.

On November 1st, 1760, the whale-bark *Ichabod* out of Nantucket, Mr John Winthrop Sloat commanding, anchored in the bay. After boarding our people, I took up my bag-pipes and climbed atop a rock and blew the Scotch air called "Flowden-Hill" and wept for my friend. M. Duclos rowed me to ship. Then Mr Sloat raised sail and carried the undefeated remnant of New France, with our arms and cannon and for colours a crimson handkerchief, in five weeks and one day to La Rochelle.

To be continued.